the Wolf Wilder

Also by

KATHERINE RUNDELL

Cartwheeling in Thunderstorms

Rooftoppers

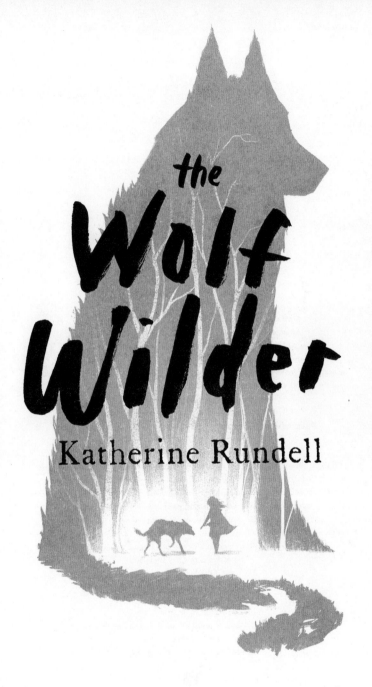

the
Wolf
Wilder

Katherine Rundell

Simon & Schuster Books for Young Readers

NEW YORK   LONDON   TORONTO   SYDNEY   NEW DELHI

SIMON & SCHUSTER BOOKS FOR YOUNG READERS
An imprint of Simon & Schuster Children's Publishing Division
1230 Avenue of the Americas, New York, New York 10020
This book is a work of fiction. Any references to historical events, real people,
or real places are used fictitiously. Other names, characters, places, and events are products
of the author's imagination, and any resemblance to actual events or places or persons,
living or dead, is entirely coincidental.
Text copyright © 2015 by Katherine Rundell
A slightly different version of this work was originally published in 2015
in Great Britain by Bloomsbury Publishing Plc.
Jacket illustration copyright © 2015 by Dan Burgess
All rights reserved, including the right of reproduction in whole or in part in any form.
SIMON & SCHUSTER BOOKS FOR YOUNG READERS is a trademark of Simon & Schuster, Inc.
For information about special discounts for bulk purchases, please contact Simon & Schuster
Special Sales at 1-866-506-1949 or business@simonandschuster.com.
The Simon & Schuster Speakers Bureau can bring authors to your live event.
For more information or to book an event, contact the Simon & Schuster Speakers Bureau
at 1-866-248-3049 or visit our website at www.simonspeakers.com.
Book design by Lizzy Bromley
The text for this book is set in Bembo.
Manufactured in the United States of America
0715 FFG
2 4 6 8 10 9 7 5 3 1
CIP data for this book is available from the Library of Congress.
ISBN 978-1-4814-1942-0
ISBN 978-1-4814-1944-4 (eBook)

To my grandmother

PAULINE BLANCHARD-SIMS,

whose flair and courage

are unrivaled

A NOTE ON WOLF WILDERS

Wolf wilders are almost impossible to spot.

A wolf wilder is not like a lion tamer nor a circus ringmaster: Wolf wilders can go their whole lives without laying eyes on a sequin. They look, more or less, like ordinary people. There are clues: More than half are missing a piece of a finger, the lobe of an ear, a toe or two. They go through clean bandages the way other people go through socks. They smell very faintly of raw meat.

In the western wild parts of Russia there are gangs of wolf merchants who hunt newborn pups. They snatch them, still wet and blind, and carry them away in boxes, selling them to men and women who live elegant lives in thick-carpeted houses in Saint Petersburg. A wolf pup can fetch a thousand rubles, a pure white one as much as twice that. A wolf in the house is said to bring good fortune: money and fame, boys with clean noses and girls without pimples. Peter the Great had seven wolves, all as white as the moon.

The captured wolves wear golden chains and are taught to sit still while people around them laugh and drink and blow cigar smoke into their eyes. They are fed caviar, which, quite reasonably, they find disgusting. Some grow so fat that the fur on their stomach sweeps the ground as they waddle up and down stairs and collects fluff and ash.

But a wolf cannot be tamed in the way a dog can be tamed, and it cannot be kept indoors. Wolves, like children, are not born to lead calm lives. Always the wolf goes mad at the imprisonment, and eventually it bites off and eats a little piece of someone who was not expecting to be eaten. The question then arises: What to do with the wolf?

Aristocrats in Russia believe that the killing of a wolf brings a unique kind of bad luck. It is not the glamorous kind of bad luck, not runaway trains and lost fortunes, but something dark and insidious. If you kill a wolf, they say, your life begins to disappear. Your child will come of age on the morning that war is declared. Your toenails will grow inward, and your teeth outward, and your gums will bleed in the night and stain your pillow red. So the wolf must not be shot, nor starved; instead, it is packed up like a parcel by nervous butlers and sent away to the wolf wilder.

The wilder will teach the wolves how to be bold again, how to hunt and fight, and how to distrust humans. They teach them how to howl, because a wolf who cannot howl is like a human who cannot laugh. And the wolves are released back onto the land they were born on, which is as tough and alive as the animals themselves.

ONE

Once upon a time, a hundred years ago, there was a dark and stormy girl.

The girl was Russian, and although her hair and eyes and fingernails were dark all the time, she was stormy only when she thought it absolutely necessary. Which was fairly often.

Her name was Feodora.

She lived in a wooden house made of timber taken from the surrounding forest. The walls were layered with sheep's wool to keep out the Russian winter, the windows were double thick, and the inside was lit with hurricane lamps. Feo had painted the lamps every color in her box of paints, so the house cast out light into the forest in reds and greens and yellows. Her mother had cut and sanded the door herself, and the wood was eight inches thick. Feo had painted it snow blue. The wolves had added claw marks over the years, which helped dissuade unwelcome visitors.

It all began—all of it—with someone knocking on the snow-blue door.

Although "knocking" was not the right word for this particular noise, Feo thought. It sounded as though someone was trying to dig a hole in the wood with his knuckles. But any knocking at all was unusual. Nobody knocked: It was just her and her mother and the wolves. Wolves do not knock. If they want to come in, they come in through the window, whether it is open or not.

Feo put down the skis she was oiling and listened. It was early, and she was still wearing her nightdress. She had no dressing gown, but she pulled on the sweater her mother had knit, which came down to the scar on her knee, and ran to the front door.

Her mother was wrapped in a bearskin housecoat, just looking up from the fire she had been lighting in the sitting room.

"I'll do it!" Feo tugged at the door with both hands. It was stiff; ice had sealed the hinges.

Her mother grabbed at her—"Wait! Feo!"

But Feo already had pulled the door open, and before she could jump back, it slapped inward, catching the side of her head.

"Ach!" Feo stumbled, and sat down on her own ankle. She said a word that made the stranger pushing his way past her raise his eyebrows and curl his lip.

The man had a face made of right angles: a jutting nose and wrinkles in angry places, deep enough to cast shadows in the dark.

"Where is Marina Petrovna?" His boots left a trail of snow down the hall.

Feo got to her knees—and then lurched back, as two more men in gray coats and black boots marched past her, missing her fingers by inches. "Move, girl." They carried between them, slung by its legs, the body of a young elk. It was dead, and dripping blood.

"Wait!" said Feo. Both wore the tall furry hats of the tsar's Imperial Army, and exaggeratedly official expressions.

Feo ran after them. She readied her elbows and knees to fight.

The two soldiers dropped the elk on the rug. The sitting room was small, and the two young men were large and mustached. Their mustaches seemed to take up most of the room.

Up close, they looked barely more than sixteen; but the

man with the door-beating fists was old, and his eyes were the oldest thing about him. Feo's stomach bunched up under her throat.

The man spoke over Feo's head to her mother. "Marina Petrovna? I am General Rakov."

"What do you want?" Marina's back was against the wall.

"I am commander of the tsar's Imperial Army for the thousand miles south of Saint Petersburg. And I am here because your wolves did this," he said. He kicked at the elk. Blood spread across his brightly polished shoe.

"*My* wolves?" Her mother's face was steady, but her eyes were neither calm nor happy. "I do not own any wolves."

"You bring them here," said Rakov. His eyes had a coldness in them you do not expect to see in a living thing. "That makes them your responsibility." His tongue was stained yellow by tobacco.

"No. No, neither of those things is true," said Feo's mother. "Other people send the wolves when they tire of them: the aristocrats, the rich. We untame them, that's all. And wolves cannot be owned."

"Lying will not help you, madam."

"I am not—"

"Those three wolves I see your child with. Those are not yours?"

"No, of course not!" began Feo. "They're—" But her mother shook her head, hard, and gestured to Feo to stay silent. Feo bit down on her hair instead, and tucked her fists into her armpits to be ready.

Her mother said, "They are hers only in the sense that I am hers and she is mine. They are Feo's companions, not her pets. But that bite isn't the work of Black or White or Gray."

"Yes. The jaw marks," said Feo. "They're from a much smaller wolf."

"You are mistaken," said Rakov, "in imagining I wish to hear excuses." His voice was growing less official: louder, ragged edged.

Feo tried to steady her breathing. The two young men, she saw, were staring at her mother: One of them had let his jaw sag open. Marina's shoulders and back and hips were wide; she had muscles that were more commonly seen on men, or rather, Feo thought, on wolves. But her face, a visitor had once said, was built on the blueprint used for snow leopards, and for saints. "The look," he had said, "is 'goddess, modified.'" Feo had pretended, at the time, not to be proud.

Rakov seemed immune to her mother's beauty. "I have been sent to collect compensation for the tsar, and I shall do that, immediately. Do not play games with me. You owe the tsar a hundred rubles."

"I don't have a hundred rubles."

Rakov slammed his fist against the wall. He was surprisingly strong for so old and shriveled a man, and the wooden walls shuddered. "Woman! I have no interest in protests or excuses. I have been sent to wrest obedience and order from this godforsaken place." He glanced down at his red-speckled shoe. "The tsar rewards success." Without warning, he kicked the elk so hard that its legs flailed, and Feo let out a hiss of horror.

"You!" The General crossed to her, leaning down until his face, veined and papery, was inches from hers. "If I had a child with a stare as insolent as yours, she would be beaten. Sit there and keep out of my sight." He pushed her backward, and the cross hanging from his neck caught in Feo's hair. He tugged it away viciously and passed through the door back into the hall. The soldiers followed him. Marina signaled to Feo to stay—the same hand gesture they used for wolves—and ran after them.

Feo crouched down in the doorway, waiting for the buzzing in her ears to die away; then she heard a cry and something breaking, and ran, skidding down the hall in her socks.

Her mother was not there, but the soldiers had crowded

into Feo's bedroom, filling her room with their smell. Feo flinched away from it: It was smoke, she thought, and a year's worth of sweat and unwashed facial hair. One of the soldiers had an underbite he could have picked his own nose with.

"Nothing worth anything," said one soldier. His eyes moved across her reindeer-skin bedspread and the hurricane lamp and came to rest on her skis, leaning against the fireplace. Feo ran to stand protectively in front of them.

"These are mine!" she said. "They're nothing to do with the tsar. I made them." It had taken her a whole month to make each ski, whittling them every evening and smoothing them with grease. Feo gripped one in both fists like a spear. She hoped the prickling in her eyes was not visible. "Get away from me."

Rakov smiled, not sweetly. He took hold of Feo's lamp, held it up to the morning light. Feo grabbed at it.

"Wait!" said Marina. She stood in the doorway. There was a bruise on her cheek that had not been there before. "Can't you see this is my daughter's room?"

The young men laughed. Rakov did not join in: He only stared at them until they turned red and fell silent. He crossed to Feo's mother, studied the mark on her cheek. He leaned forward until the tip of his nose was touching her skin, and sniffed. Marina stood motionless, her lips bitten shut. Then Rakov grunted and threw the lamp at the ceiling.

"*Chyort!*" cried Feo, and ducked. Broken glass rained down on her shoulders. She lunged forward at the general, swinging blindly with her ski. "Get out!" she said. "Get out!"

The general laughed, caught the ski, and wrenched it from her. "Sit down and behave, before you make me angry."

"Get *out*," said Feo.

"Sit! Or you will end up in the same position as that elk."

Marina seemed to jerk into life. "*What?* What insanity in your head makes you think you can threaten my child?"

"You *both* disgust me." Rakov shook his head. "It is an abomination to live with those animals. Wolves are vermin with teeth."

"That is . . ." Feo's mother's face spoke a hundred different swearwords before she said, "Inaccurate."

"And your daughter is vermin when she is with those wolves. I've heard stories about you both—you're unfit to be a mother."

Marina let out a sound that it hurt Feo to hear, partway between a gasp and a hiss.

He went on. "There are schools—in Vladivostok—where

she could learn the values of a better mother—Mother Russia. Perhaps I will have her sent there."

"Feo," said Marina, "go and wait in the kitchen. *Immediately*, please." Feo darted out, rounded the door and stopped there, hesitating, peering through the crack in the hinge. Her mother's face, as she turned to Rakov, was shining with anger and with other, more complicated things.

"Feo is *my child*. For God's sake, do you not know what that means?" Marina shook her head incredulously. "She's worth an entire army of men like you, and my love for her is a thing you should underestimate only if you have a particularly powerful death wish. The love of a parent for a child—it *burns*."

"How inconvenient for you!" Rakov ran a hand along his chin. "What is your point?" He wiped his boot on the bed. "And make it quick, you're becoming tedious."

"My point is that you will keep your hands off my daughter if you value their current position at the ends of your arms."

Rakov snorted. "That is somewhat unfeminine."

"Not at all. It seems profoundly feminine to me."

Rakov stared at Marina's fingers, the tips of two of which were missing, and then at her face. His expression was frightening: There was something uncontained about it. Marina stared back at him. Rakov blinked first.

He grunted, and strode out the door. Feo twisted backward out of his way, then ran after him into the kitchen.

"You are not making this easy for yourself," he said. His face was dispassionate as he gripped the side of the dining table and overturned it. Feo's favorite mug crashed on the floor.

"Mama!" said Feo. She took a handful of her mother's coat as Marina swept into the room, and held it tight.

Rakov did not even glance in her direction. "Take the paintings," he said. They had three, each with boldly colored cubes arranged in shapes that hinted at men and women. Marina loved them. Feo humored her.

"Wait, don't!" said Feo. "That's Mama's Malevich. It was a present! Wait! Here. There's this!" Feo fished her gold chain from around her neck and held it out to the youngest soldier. "It's gold. It was Mama's mother's before it was mine, so it's old. Gold's worth more when it's old." The soldier bit the chain, sniffed it, nodded, and handed it to Rakov.

Feo ran to open the front door. She stood by it, the snow blowing in and coating her socks. Her whole body was shaking. "Now you have to go."

Marina closed her eyes for one brief moment, then

opened them and smiled at Feo. The two soldiers spat on the floor in a bored kind of way and headed out into the snow.

"This is the only warning you will be given," said Rakov. He ignored the open door and the snow-covered wind. "The tsar's orders. The tsar will not have his animals slaughtered by wolves *you* have taught to hunt. From now on, if the people of the city send you wolves, you shoot them."

"No!" said Feo. "We can't! Anyway, we don't have a gun! Tell him, Mama!"

Rakov ignored her. "You will send back a message to the superstitious idiots who send their ridiculous pets to you that you have released them into the wild, and then you will shoot the animals."

"I will not," said Marina. Her face looked empty of blood. It made Feo's stomach ache; it made her wish that she had a gun to point at the man in the doorway.

Rakov's coat wrinkled as he shrugged. "You know the penalty for those who act against the orders of the tsar? You remember what happened to the rioters in Saint Petersburg? This is the only warning you will receive." He crossed to the front door, and as he passed he pointed a gloved finger at Feo's heart. "You too, girl." He jabbed once, hard, against her collarbone. Feo jumped backward.

"If we see that child with a wolf, we'll shoot the wolf and take the child."

He slammed the door behind him.

Later that day Feo and her mother sat by the fire. The shards of broken glass and china had been swept clear and the elk had been packed in ice and stored in the woodshed—Feo had wanted to bury it properly, with a cross and a funeral, but her mother had said no: They might need to eat it if the winter kept marching on. Feo rested her head on her mother's shoulder.

"What do we do now, Mama?" she asked. "Now they've said we have to kill the wolves? We won't, will we? I won't let you."

"No, *lapushka*!" Marina's arm, with its embroidery of scars and muscle, enwrapped Feo. "Of course not. But we'll be a little more silent, and a little more watchful." She rattled the chestnuts roasting in the grate, and flipped one into Feo's hands. "It's what the wolves do. We can do it too. Can't we?"

Of course they could, Feo thought that evening as she put on her skis. Humans, on the whole, Feo could take or leave; there was only one person she loved properly, with the sort of fierce pride that gets people into trouble, or prison, or history books. Her mother, she thought, could do anything.

It took Feo ten minutes to ski to the ruins of the stone chapel. At the entrance hall were three dilapidated statues of saints: They had no heads, and two of them had grown a scaly skin of green lichen. Even without heads, the saints managed to look unimpressed by this state of affairs. Only two and a half of the chapel walls were still standing, and the roof had long ago crumbled onto the mosaic floor below. There were pews, half eaten away by woodworm, and a marble miniature of the Virgin, which Feo had cleaned with the chewed end of a twig. If the light was right in the chapel, and if you looked closely, you could see that the walls had once been painted with gold figures. It was, Feo thought, the most beautiful place on earth.

In the chapel lived a pack of three wolves.

One wolf was white, one black, and one a grayish mix, with black ears and the face of a politician. They could not be called tame—they certainly would not come if you called—but nor were they wholly wild. And Feo, the neighbors said, was half feral herself, and they looked in horror at her wolf-smelling red cloak. It made sense, then, that Feo and the wolves would be best friends: They met each other halfway.

As she skied in through the door, the wolves were chewing on the carcasses of two ravens, covering the statue of Mary with flecks of blood. Feo did not go close—it is wisest not to interrupt wolves when they are eating, even if they are your best friends—but waited, her feet tucked up on one of the pews, until they had finished. They were unhurried, licking their muzzles and forepaws, and then charged at her as a gang, knocking her off the pew and covering her chin and hands with wolf spit. She and Black had a game of chase in and out of the pews, Feo swinging for balance around the headless saints. She felt some of the gray weight of the day lift off her stomach.

Feo could not remember a time when she had not known and loved the wolves. It was impossible not to love them: They were so lean and beautiful and uncompromising. She had grown up picking pine needles out of their fur and old meat from their teeth. She could howl, her mother used to say, before she could talk. Wolves made sense to her; wolves were one of the few things worth dying for. It seemed unlikely, though, that anyone would ask her to: After all, wolves were, in general, on the other side of the equation.

TWO

The wolf who arrived two weeks after the general's warning was a young one, a female with a beautiful tail, but fatter than any wolf should be.

Usually, when the carriages arrived at the house in the woods, the drivers would blink, looking around for someone large and male to come and untie the wolf. Instead, they would see Feo and her mother coming from the house, wrapped in cooking smells. Marina was thirty-three and tall as the lintel on the front door. She had taught Feo to do pull-ups on the cottage door frames. She had a four-clawed scar circling her left eye. Men who met her had been known to forget, just for a second, how to breathe.

This morning, though, Feo greeted the cart alone. She

took the struggling wolf in her arms, nudging away the driver's offer of help, and laid her in the snow. She stroked her head, and she quieted.

The wolf's fur was the blackest Feo had ever seen. At night she would be invisible—in fact darker than the night itself, because Russian nights, especially when there is snow to reflect the stars, are never absolutely dark.

"Good to meet you," said Feo to the wolf. She ignored the driver and dipped her face, touching her nose to the wolf's muzzle. The wolf licked her chin. Her breath smelled reassuringly of spit and silver coins, but the long tongue was swollen and bleeding a little.

"She's bitten herself," said Feo. "You should have driven her more carefully." She looked properly at the driver. He was a big man, with long nose hair that blended seamlessly into his beard. "Did you pass any soldiers on the way?"

"What? Why would I—"

"Nothing, in that case." Feo shook her head, hard. "Forget I said that." She untied the wolf softly, keeping her hands where the wolf could see them. Her claws were too long, starting to curl inward toward the pads of her feet. Feo took her knife, balanced one of the wolf's paws on her knee and began to cut the claws.

"Have you got any food for her?" Feo asked the driver. "She's hungry."

"No." He raised his eyebrows. "She's fat enough already."

Feo braced the wolf's jaw open against her torso and ran her fingers along the teeth, pushing at the gums.

"You—little girl, stop that! Mother of God!" The man let out an impressive cascade of swearwords. Feo noticed with interest that his fingernails were sweating. "Do you want to be killed? What are you *doing*?"

"I'm checking for gum decay." There was none. She let the wolf go and scratched her under the front legs. The wolf collapsed on her side, whimpering with pleasure.

The man still looked horrified, and almost angry. "Shouldn't that thing have a bit of rope around its jaws?" He was staring at Feo, at her eyes and at her earlobe: It had been split in two by a wolf's accidental claw when she was six. Feo shook her hair over her face and gave him a withering look. At least, she tried to. She had only read about it in books and wasn't sure how it was done. She imagined it involved a lot of nostril work.

"Wolves don't wear rope. They're not like *dogs*." They had more fire in them, she thought, and uneven tempers. It was difficult to explain. She bit her lip, thinking how to put it, then shook her head. Other people were so difficult. "You could go, if you felt like you wanted to. That's how I'd feel if I were you."

Marina emerged from the house, her hair half braided, just in time to see the cart disappearing.

"He didn't want a drink?" she asked.

"No," said Feo. She grinned at her mother. "He didn't seem that keen on staying, actually."

"That's probably just as well. Come, quickly—let's get her under the trees and out of sight."

"You think they're watching us?" Feo stared around at the snow.

"It's possible, *lapushka*. I don't think it was an empty threat. Empty threats, in my experience, involve fewer breakages."

The wolf walked agonizingly slowly toward the woods, and she yelped as she went, as if unfamiliar with cold.

Marina dusted snow from Feo's hair. "We need to talk about what might happen."

"Uh-huh." The wolf was coughing. Feo laid two fingers on her throat and kneaded gently. "What did she do, do you think? Why did they send her away?"

"They said she got into the countess's wardrobe and chewed up the dresses. But are you listening to me?"

"That's *all*? She didn't bite anyone? Yes, sorry, I'm listening!" Feo thought about her pack. Gray had bitten off the thumb of a visiting tax collector. White had scraped a cut an inch deep in a duchess's thigh when she had tried to make the wolf dance for visitors. And Black had eaten three toes, which, technically, had belonged to an English lord. Her wolves, Feo thought, were a bunch of the most beautiful criminals.

"If Rakov's men are watching us, you can't be seen with the wolves in public."

"Of course. You already said that, Mama! And I asked the driver if he saw any soldiers, and he said no."

"You did *what*?" Marina looked startled. "My darling, you mustn't mention soldiers to anybody. It's not wise to let strangers know you have anything to fear."

"Oh." Feo's insides felt suddenly a little tighter, a little hotter. "I'm sorry. I didn't know that."

"It's my fault. I should have warned you." Marina rubbed both hands through her hair. "I've been making an escape plan. Just in case."

The wolf set the side of her muzzle against Feo's knee and coughed. "Mama, did she swallow the dresses? If she's still got material in her teeth, it could be hurting her."

"Feo, leave the—"

"Look, Mama." Feo pushed open the wolf's jaws. Wolf spit covered her hand as she felt carefully inside. At the back of the wolf's mouth a wedge of cloth had stuck between the teeth. Feo tugged. It was red velvet, with one tiny seed pearl surviving of the embroidery.

"There! And also this thread they used to tie her is too thin," said Feo. She held up the wolf's paw for her mother to see. "Look! Blood, there, see? Her paws are so fragile." She kissed the wolf's ear. "We should call you Tenderfoot."

"Here, I've got some ointment." Marina bent and rubbed some brownish paste onto the wolf's paw. Her hands were faster than most people's, and the wolf relaxed into her grip. "But, Feo, do you understand? You'll need to pack a bag—food, dry clothes, a knife, rope—and keep it by the back door, just in case."

Feo dragged her attention away from Tenderfoot. "In case what, though, Mama?"

"In case Rakov comes back for us."

"But he wouldn't! Would he? I mean—he's old." Feo tried to push away the memory of his eyes staring out at her from the yellowed face. "Old people like sitting down. And growing ear hair. And . . . soup." Feo had met very few old people. "He'll be busy doing those things."

Marina smiled, but the corners of her mouth looked heavy. "Just keep your eyes open, *lapushka*. If you want to see the wolves, stay in the chapel or behind the house. We'll wild this one as quickly as we can and release her at the woods to the west, by the kidney-shaped lake, so she won't stray near Rakov."

"But those woods are bad for hunting! She'll starve!"

"Not if we teach her to catch birds. Besides, wolves find a way. Wolves are the witches of the animal world."

THREE

Feo had been wilding wolves alone since she was ten years old, but never had she had to do it in secret, never with the back of her neck prickling. Wilding is best done alone, and Marina left her to attend to a sick dog ten miles off: Wilders in Russia often doubled as vets. But her face, as she went, was unsettled.

"Keep your knife sharp, keep your eyes sharper, my darling," she said. "Remember that."

Now Feo crouched in the snow in front of Tenderfoot. The days had grown bruisingly cold, and her breath together with the wolf's formed a cloud around their heads. "Are you ready?" she asked.

She knew the wilding stages: She had recited them before bed since she was four. "First," she whispered to herself, "ascertain what world the wolf has come from." Some of the wolves who came to them were manic and snappish, and took very little time to rewild. Some were timid and jumpy and barely able to walk.

"Sit," she said to the wolf. Tenderfoot sat, carefully, her four feet arranged as neat as a laid-out table.

"Down. Lie down." Tenderfoot lay down in the snow. She did not take her eyes off Feo.

"Paw?" Feo asked.

The wolf sat up, licked her paw with exquisite courtesy, and held it out to Feo. Feo did not take it.

"Beg?"

Tenderfoot twitched, then hesitated. The expression in her eyes was mutinous. Feo grimaced. She tried to make her voice aristocratic. "Beg!"

The wolf rose instantly onto her hind legs and lolled her tongue. Her face was that of a duchess on finding a dead rat under the bed.

Feo laughed. "Yes, I know." "Society" wolves could always beg, hold out a paw, lie still. Often—it made Feo want to cry—they could dance on their hind legs, their faces blank.

"Once," she said to Tenderfoot, "we had a brown alpha—sort of tawny colored—who could pull the trigger of a rifle with his nose. Which is a *ridiculous* thing to teach him. As if a wolf needs a gun."

Usually she would test if the wolf could howl, but that, she thought, would be as obvious as writing out an invitation to Rakov. "We need to be quiet, if we can." She pulled Tenderfoot closer to a tree and said, "Sit, for now."

Feo sat too in the ankle-deep snow. Her cloak had an oilskin finish that kept the cold out, more or less. It was secondhand and much too long, but her mother had pinned it up so that it swirled around her ankles when she ran.

"I *wish* they wouldn't teach you to beg. It's . . ." Feo hesitated: It was like telling a god to clean his shoes. "It makes me want to bite. Stupid people." She looked inside the wolf's ears. "Stupid rich people."

There was the sound behind them of falling snow. Feo whipped round.

"Hello?" she called. "Who's there?" and then, "I can see you! Come out!"

There was silence.

"If you're watching, you need to know that I have a knife. And an angry wolf." Tenderfoot tucked her nose inside Feo's armpit and whimpered.

"She's more murderous than she looks," Feo called into the silence.

One of the trees scattered its load of snow onto the ground below, and a crow as big as Feo's head took off from the branches. Feo held her breath, but nothing else moved. She stood and looked around for footprints. The snow was wind churned, but she could see no footmarks. She crouched down again, her heart beating a little faster.

"*Stupid*," said Feo again. Tenderfoot's hackles were on end. Feo smoothed them down. "We're all right, I think. Shh, *lapushka*. I won't let anyone hurt you."

She tugged the wolf to her feet. "Come, we'll find you a good tree. I'll show you how wolves build their dens."

She led the wolf to where the trees were thickest, and began to pile the snow. As she worked, Feo told the wolf about the land around her new home.

Feo's part of Russia was a place that the world had, by and large, decided to pass by. The hilltops absorbed the cold, and the snow there lay thicker and stiffer than anywhere for a hundred miles. If you stood on the tallest hill and looked to the north, there the woods, hills, and the stone barracks of the soldiers. The soldiers used to be a bunch of harmless drunks, sent into the countryside to be out of the way; but since Rakov's arrival, Feo had heard regimental orders shouted on the wind. Sometimes at night there were screams. Beyond the soldiers' gray buildings was flat countryside, snow-covered fields and trees, and then, far off and merging with the clouds, the smoke of Saint Petersburg.

"See?" said Feo to the black wolf. "And to the south there's just snow and snow, and then, see here if you squint"—she shielded the wolf's eyes with her hand—"more snow."

Feo loved it. The land around the house shook and shone with life. She had seen people pass by her wood bewailing the sameness of the white landscape, but they were just illiterate: They hadn't learned how to read the world properly. The snow gossiped and hinted of storms and birds. It told a new story every morning. Feo grinned, and sniffed the sharpness of the air. "It's the most talkative weather there is," she told Tenderfoot.

Her world was not, of course, all perfect. The few children in the farms were much older than her—almost grown up, with the beginnings of beards—or too young, and liable to cry and vomit unreasonably if she came near with the wolf pack. Feo liked the look of some of the older ones, but they laughed when she tried to join them, and said she was a child and smelled of wolves.

Feo found it hard to act normally around strangers. She would be too silent, or rough when she'd hoped to be funny.

For weeks and months after, some of the things she had said would come back to her and she would have to bury her head in the snow to cool down her cheeks. Adults, in Feo's experience, often backed away when they met her. Her mother said it might—possibly—be because she stared at them. But the wolves stared too, and nobody reprimanded *them*.

And the wolves were enough. They were better than enough. And two of the wolves, as Feo pointed out whenever her mother became anxious about her possible loneliness, were technically girls of about her own age. "I know they don't speak Russian," said Feo, "but that doesn't mean we don't understand each other."

White was the acknowledged beauty of the pack, and when Feo buried her face in the wolf's neck, the fur was so soft it felt almost wet. She was young and, the male wolves who passed through seemed to agree, glamorous. Her snout was narrow enough to fit inside Feo's ear. Most wolves are born with blue eyes, which turn yellow or gold at three months; White's had remained blue.

And there was Gray. Gray was a few months older than Feo, and Marina had fought a wolf hunter for her when she was a newborn pup cut from the stomach of her mother, a fight that had ended in a broken nose for Marina and a week in the hospital for the hunter. Perhaps because her first day on earth had been so stressful, Gray's temper was large and unwieldy. The flick of her ears suggested she was invincible. Feo was not afraid of Gray because Feo refused, on principle, to be afraid of any animal—but if she'd had to be, it would definitely have been Gray she would have chosen.

"It's hard to be absolutely sure," Feo told Black, "that she's not going to bite off some part of me I'd rather keep."

Black had been sold for four thousand rubles because of the beauty of his coat, and until he found Feo, he had loved nobody. When he first came to the cabin in the woods, he had been fat, with a bottom large enough to block a doorway. Now, though, he was awe-inspiring, and the best friend anybody could dream of. On his hind legs, Black was tall enough to make two Feos, and—she knew from experience—his paws were as big as Feo's face. But Black was lightning quick.

To see a wolf run, Feo reckoned, is to see something extraordinary—because, she told Tenderfoot, "a real wolf runs in the way that a thunderstorm would run if it had legs. That's what you're aiming for, all right?"

Feo straightened up and rubbed Tenderfoot's ears. The wolf flinched and whined.

"*Lapushka*, you look like you wouldn't know where to find your own teeth."

Many of the wolves who came to them, captured at birth and kept on chains, had never run farther than the length of a drawing room.

"We're going to do some running now," said Feo. "Do you know running? It's like walking, only more of it."

Tenderfoot stepped into a dip in the ground, found the snow was suddenly up to her stomach, and collapsed in a panicked heap, her head tucked down to her stomach. Feo reached into the snow, found the wolf's belly, and pulled her to her feet. She weighed as much as Feo herself.

"Wolves," she said, "are supposed to be bold, and gallant, and fierce." She rubbed Tenderfoot's ears. "You might need to work on that." Feo tightened the leather straps of her skis, wiped the icy mist off her hair before it could turn solid, and tucked it down her back inside her shirt. "Follow me, now!"

She pushed forward and dropped off the edge of the hill. The sound of the wind in the trees made it difficult to tell if the wolf was following, but usually they came stumbling after her instinctively. Feo turned. The wolf sat at the top of the hill peering down, a dinner-party expression on her face.

Feo bit away the solid snot icing on her lip, spat it out, and stamped, crisscrossing with her skis, back up the hill.

"You're very beautiful, you know, but you have the

instincts of a carpet," said Feo. "Come on! We're trying to do this quickly! Mama's worried." She took a bone from her pocket and skied in a circle around the wolf. "Come on, Tenderfoot!"

Feo reached the lip of the hill and tipped backward over the edge. The wolf followed, not neatly or gracefully, but at least she was running. They made half a mile's worth of slow progress before the wolf stopped, turned once in a circle, and fell asleep.

Feo grinned, and clamped a fist over Tenderfoot's jaw and shook it gently. "Wake up! This isn't the place for sleeping. You were very good, though, for a beginner. Here." She held out the bone. The wolf's tongue was rough and hungry against her palm.

As Tenderfoot chewed, Feo felt the hairs lift along her arms and the base of her neck, and for a moment she was unsure why. She laid a hand on the wolf's neck; with the other she felt at her waist for her knife. It came again: a smell in the wind. "Just an elk," she said out loud. "A damp elk." But it smelled, in fact, of damp human clothing. She stared around the clearing: only snow and sky, turning the slanting pinks of sunset.

She straightened up. "Quick. We need to hide you for the night."

Usually, the wolves who came to be made wild slept under the trees. But since Rakov's visit, Mama said, everything had to be different.

"Come." Feo led the wolf up to the house, glancing over her shoulder every other step, trying to keep her back to the trees. "Hurry. We'll put you by the stove, just for tonight. You must try not to eat the cutlery. We had a wolf once who ate all the forks. It gave him indigestion."

FOUR

The next day was a day of discoveries. Feo discovered two things: that the wolf was not fat and that the world was not safe.

Feo was running through the woods, one hand on Tenderfoot's neck, looking out for squirrels. They saw a jackdaw poking hopefully in the snow.

"That's food, Tenderfoot! Food, quick!"

Several things happened at once. The wolf gave a howl of terror at the sight of the bird. The side of her belly moved and pulsed. And a person fell out of a tree, pointed a pistol at Feo's head, and said, "Put your hands where I can see them."

Feo jerked to a stop. Very slowly—so slowly, she hoped,

that he would not notice she was moving—she inched to stand in front of the wolf.

"Hands up!"

Feo put her hands up. "Who are you?" An unfamiliar dizzy panic swept over her. She tried to shove the wolf's great bulk behind her knees, out of sight.

"I'm a soldier. In the Imperial Army."

Feo swallowed. Terror bleached right through her, and she lowered one hand to take hold of Tenderfoot's neck, just in case she tried to run near that gun. "Don't move, *lapushka*," she whispered. *"Stay."*

"*Both* hands up!" said the soldier.

"If you try to shoot her," Feo said, "I'll kill you."

"Will you?" said the soldier. He came a step closer, gun outstretched. "I don't see how."

"I will! Get back, I swear I'll bite you!" The soldier stopped, his face astonished. Feo breathed in. "If you come a step closer, I'll pull your fingers out."

The soldier looked interested, despite himself. "Could you actually do that?" His face, twisted in curiosity, looked younger than she had expected.

"Yes," lied Feo. And then: "Probably, actually. If you stayed still." She stepped forward. He didn't move. Her hands were shaking, so she hid them behind her back. "I mean

it, though—don't point that at us!" He still didn't move.
"Mama says pointing a gun is a failure of imagination."
She gestured with her elbow at Tenderfoot. "And I have
a wolf."

"I know. I've been watching." The soldier picked some
pine needles from his uniform and brushed the snow from
his hair. His voice was too high for an adult's, she thought. A
boy's voice. "She's not notably fierce, is she?"

Feo was surprised by how annoyed she felt. "She's
much better than yesterday already! Yesterday you wouldn't
have been surprised if she'd started knitting. And besides,"
she added, speaking the thing she had just realized, "she's
pregnant. You can't shoot a pregnant wolf. You can't kill
something before it's had a chance to try out life."

"I have to." The boy rubbed his arms. He was tall and
fair, and without the covering of snow he looked very thin;
the bones in his hands seemed to be making a bid to escape
from his skin. His voice sounded of cities: *Soft*, Feo thought.
He didn't look very soldierly. "It's unfortunate, but there's
nothing I can do. Rules have to be followed."

"No, they don't." Feo risked another step toward him.
"Please. Really, they don't."

"They'll punish me if I don't."

"Well, I—I'll wolf you if you do." But she sounded only

slightly less frightened than she felt. She kept one hand on Tenderfoot.

The boy shook his head. "I'm the one with the gun here. One gun beats one wolf."

That was so obviously true that Feo could do nothing but scowl. "Who'll punish you, though?" Feo thought she might know. "General Rakov?"

"Don't say that so loud!" The boy looked around as if expecting Rakov to spring out from behind a squirrel. "Yes, *him*."

"What does he do?"

"*He* doesn't do much personally, not usually. But. He likes to watch."

"Oh," said Feo. There was something terrible in the boy's voice: She hadn't realized it was possible to fit so much fear into so few words.

"He makes his officers bring us to his study. I bled for three days once." The boy twitched his shoulders, as if shaking something off. "Look—I *have* to shoot the wolf. It doesn't matter if I *want* to. You don't understand: There are six of us on watch, and if I don't catch you, someone else will."

"What!" Feo stared around the clearing. The air was still. "Where?" She should have brought more than one knife, she thought. It was a stupid mistake.

"Not here. We're spaced over twenty miles. Anyone wolf wilding is to be arrested, Rakov said. Wolves are to be shot. Those were the orders."

"I wasn't wilding. I was just playing."

"You don't look the sort of person who just plays." As he said it, there was a rustle of branches far off. The boy cried out—a short, sharp shriek, quickly stifled—and Feo saw Black's back as he streaked past among the trees, heading toward her.

"Oh no." Feo whispered the strongest of the swearwords she had learned from the driver the day before.

"Is that—"

"Go, Black!" she called. She pointed away, toward the chapel, but the wolf kept coming. "Black, please, go! He's got a gun!"

The boy raised his pistol.

"No!" said Feo. "Go back!" She couldn't move from Tenderfoot's side, but she spat at the boy. He jumped back, but only a step: not enough. "Listen, if you shoot him, I'll find where you sleep and come after you in the night." The boy's eyes were widening. "I will! That's not a joke."

Black erupted from the trees, growling. The boy cried out. Feo threw herself over Tenderfoot's belly and screwed her eyes shut, but the pistol did not fire. She opened them:

The boy stood where he was, frozen. The pistol in his hand was shaking.

Black slid to a halt in the snow and rested his head against Feo's thigh. He must have picked up the tension, the shiver in her skin, because another growl came from his throat.

"Oh dear," said Feo.

"What's going on?" asked the boy.

"He doesn't like you."

"Why not?"

"Because I don't like you. And he can feel it."

"Well, stop it!"

"Disliking you?"

"Yes! Now! Stop it immediately!"

"You *very* much started it! You're pointing a gun at me!"

"I order you to control that wolf!"

"I can't! That's the point. He might do what I ask, but he might not. He's not a *pet*." She shouted the final word, and Black growled again. The sound shook snow from the trees above them.

The boy, Feo saw, was shaking like a whole forest of leaves. "Don't let it come nearer!"

"Put your gun down, then!" Feo decided to risk it: She turned her back on him and knelt in the snow. "Hush, all right?" She put a hand on each side of Black's face and breathed warm air onto his nose. "We're all right, *cherniy*. There's no need to eat anybody today." She glanced round at the boy.

He was standing with his fists balled tight, but his gun was in the snow.

"I'll let you know if that changes," she said to Black. The wolf wouldn't understand the words, but the sound—the softness, a whisper—reassured him, and the hackles along his back dropped down.

There was the sound of a throat being ostentatiously cleared. "So—what now?" said the boy.

"Now you swear never to tell anyone you saw us," said Feo. She tried to put toughness and growl into her voice. "Unless you want to find a wolf under your bed, eating your toes."

"Look, I'm supposed to arrest you," he said. "If they find out I saw you and didn't take you, they'd . . ."

"What? What would they do?"

"Honestly, you don't want to know what they'd do."

"No, I do. A bit."

"You don't. They always say the Russian army wasn't built on compliments and milk. I *have* to arrest you. All right? I'm going to, right now. Are you ready?" He drew himself up to his full height, which was at least a foot taller than Feo.

Feo looked hard at him, at the way he stood, at the skin around his eyes and on his wrists. Wrist skin is very revealing, of many things. "You're the same age as me."

"I'm not! I'm thirteen: nearly fourteen."

"That's still not old enough to arrest anybody."

"I'm supposed to call the others. I have a whistle, here." He gestured to the inside of his coat. "I'm going to do it now. I have to." He began to fumble with the gold buttons on the front of his coat.

At that moment Tenderfoot, who had been hunkered low, panting next to Black, created a diversion. She tipped onto her side and gave a short, guttural howl.

"Oh no!" The swoop Feo's heart gave had nothing to do with the boy or the gun. "Tenderfoot!"

"What's happening?"

"Be quiet!" said Feo. "She needs to concentrate."

"Why?"

"Hush!" Feo knelt.

"Is she taking some kind of test?"

"She's giving birth!" Feo laid a hand on the wolf's pulsing belly. "Hush, *lapushka*. Good girl. You're safe, I promise." She laid a hand on the wolf's muzzle to check her breathing. It was ragged, and Tenderfoot's muscles were tight, and there was urgency in her eyes. She was panting.

"Right now?" said the boy. He edged closer. "How long will it take?"

"Keep back, please. She doesn't need you breathing all over her. And yes, obviously, right now."

The soldierly pose disappeared. The boy who took a step forward was just a boy. "Can I watch?"

"Only if you give me that gun."

He hesitated. "But you'll—"

"I won't shoot you with it. Probably. But you can't be near us with a gun. Nobody is allowed to be near a pregnant wolf with a gun." She tried to say it as if it were a law, rather than something she had just made up.

He barely hesitated before he picked the gun out of the snow and tossed it, barrel first, toward her. Feo caught it, sniffed it, and threw it deep into the woods.

"You can come this close," said Feo, and she drew a line in the snow, "but not closer." She turned her back on him: The boy could wait. There were more important things.

Tenderfoot's breath was coming in snuffles that blew the snow around her muzzle into flurries.

The boy edged closer and knelt, two wolves' breadths away from the girl. "Is it painful?" he asked. "She looks in pain."

"Of course it's painful!" said Feo. "But less bad than for humans, Mama says. Because their heads are smaller."

"Can I do anything to help? I'm Ilya, by the way."

"No. Not yet, anyway. You can stay back."

"You're supposed to say your name now. The other soldiers say you and your mother are *socially malnourished*."

"Can't you just be quiet? This is important!"

"I know your name, anyway. It's Feodora."

Feo ignored him: She ignored anyone who called her by her full name. It was a policy.

Tenderfoot gave a breathy howl where she lay, and a tiny parcel of fur and slime landed in the snow. Feo held her breath, unsure what to do. The parcel was not moving. Tenderfoot twisted round to sniff at it, licked it. Then she turned away. The noise that came from her was more of a wail than a growl.

"What now?" said Ilya.

"I don't know! All right?" Feo picked up the little parcel of wet fur. It was much too small, and much too still. She licked the hem of her cloak and very gently rubbed the furry body. Nothing happened. She touched it with a fingertip. There was no heartbeat.

"Is everything working?" said Ilya.

"No, it's not!" said Feo. Frantically, she opened the pup's tiny mouth with her little finger and breathed in a puff of air. It did not move. Already the body was growing cold.

"What's happened?"

"They've been feeding her the wrong things." She dug her nails into her palms. "It's dead."

"Dead!" He looked stricken. "Already? Can't we—"

"No. It was dead in the womb. It's too small: You can see." She ducked her head, hiding behind her hair so he couldn't see that her face was wet. "People don't know how to feed wolves. *Idiots*."

There was more straining coming from the wolf, and a strange whining noise Feo had never heard a wolf make.

"Wait! There's another! Be quiet while she pushes!" Feo stroked Tenderfoot's head and peered at her hind end. "Well done, *lapushka*! Steady, now. You can do this."

"What's happening?" hissed Ilya.

"Which part of 'be quiet or the wolves will eat you' have you not understood?" said Feo. Her chest was burning: She realized she'd been holding her breath. She gulped in air, and then: "Sorry. I'm not—she needs quiet." She stroked the fur along the wolf's spine and prayed to whichever saint took care of wolf pups and vulnerable, snuffling things.

Tenderfoot strained again, and the lump that slid into Feo's waiting hands was bigger, and wriggling hard.

"It's alive!" said Ilya. "I can see, it's alive!"

Feo beamed down into the snow. "Yes! But don't jinx it!

Wait for a moment." She set the pup down by Tenderfoot's mouth.

The new mother licked it clean. Wolves do not purr, but they do vibrate with pleasure. Tenderfoot was vibrating now. She laid the parcel on Feo's knees.

Ilya gave a squeak. "Look at that!"

The parcel moved. It gave a cough, no louder than the rustling of paper. Feo could feel, through her skirt, its fingernail-size beating heart.

"Oh!" said Feo. She bent her head to whisper. "Welcome to the world, little one." It was like being given a kingdom.

"Did you see that?" said Ilya. "She gave him to you!"

"It's what they do in a pack. They raise the pups together."

The look on the boy's face was so exactly like Black's when food was nearby that Feo was startled: His expression was hungry, and full of longing. She shifted in the snow to make room for him. "Here. Come and see."

"It's blind!" he gasped. "Feodora, help it!"

"It's not blind. I mean—it's supposed to be. They don't open their eyes for about ten days."

The pup's hips stuck up in two sharp points, as did his shoulders. He was black with white toes, and with smudges of gray on his chest. His eyes were closed, and as soon as Feo placed him at Tenderfoot's nipple, his paws began to scrabble at her stomach, blindly coaxing out the milk. Feo laughed. It looked, irresistibly, like an old man dancing.

Ilya put out a hand to touch the pup, then hesitated, retracted it, sat on it. "Look at that," he breathed. "The cub's drinking, isn't it?"

"Pup," said Feo. "Wolf babies are pups."

"No more flesh on him than a kitchen table," said Ilya. Feo stared, and he blushed. "That's what my mother said about me when I was born. Before she died, not afterward. My father said it'd be useful to have a thin child: less to feed." He moved closer.

Feo wasn't sure what to say. The boy wasn't looking at her. He was looking at the pup, who was accidentally tasting snow for the first time. The pup sneezed: tiny, doll-size sneezes.

She said, "I'm Feo, actually. Not Feodora."

"Feo. Can I touch it, Feo?"

"*Him.* He's a boy. It's really up to Tenderfoot, not me." But Ilya's face was so hopeful it hurt her chest to look at him, and she shrugged. "If you make sure she can always see your hands, she won't bite. They get nervous when they can't see both your hands."

He quivered from boots to cap as he stroked the pup. Feo watched him. His eyelashes were so blond they were almost invisible, and they were covered in snow. There was a scar on one eyelid.

"The General wanted us to shoot *this*?" he asked. "He said wolves were vicious."

"He's afraid," said Feo. "Fear is as dangerous as hatred sometimes. Animals know that."

"But look at his claws!" said Ilya. Feo looked: They were short and thin as fingernail clippings. Ilya touched the pup's paws with the tip of his little finger. "You couldn't shoot a wolf pup," he said. "It's only just begun."

They sat, wolves and children jumbled together, for hours. They didn't speak much: They just watched the pup staggering between his mother's nipples, and clambering over the mountain of her side, and sliding off into the snow.

It was dusk when Feo roused her pack. Tenderfoot lifted her pup in her mouth and looked to the girl for directions.

"We have to go," said Feo. "Good night."

"Where are you taking her?"

Feo hesitated. "You won't tell?"

"Never! Really, I swear, Feo."

"I'm taking her home: my house. She can sleep inside if she wants to, or on the porch. Will they see us, between the wood and the house?"

"No. I'm covering these six miles." He looked down at

the gold buttons on his sleeve. "Can I come back?"

"Won't they beat you?"

He shrugged. "Can I come back?"

"All right. Yes. If you want."

"And help with the wilding?"

"It's not easy." Feo fought down her grin. It was too early, she reckoned, to be grinning at soldiers. "You can, but not if you bring a gun. And only if you promise never to tell what you saw. On pain of death by wolf."

"That seems fair enough," he said. "I mean"—and the city twang she had heard before was in his voice again—"if you had to die, at least that way would be exciting."

FIVE

The weeks that followed were some of the happiest of Feo's life. They stayed close to the house, as far away from the soldiers' barracks as possible. Marina patrolled the area, her knife always at her side, her face pinched, but no gray coats appeared. And the pup, even before his eyes opened, was evidently an animal of fearsome intelligence—when he was awake, which was not often. He slept next to Tenderfoot outside the front door. Feo would sit on her windowsill at sunrise with the pup in her lap while Tenderfoot nosed around the snow, darting around corners, lunging at puffs of wind, chewing the side of the house, disappearing for an hour or two, trying out her new running legs.

Sometimes Ilya turned up without warning. He tried, at first, to make it seem as if he had stumbled up the hill by accident and was surprised to find Feo chopping wood or oiling her skis.

Feo laughed. "Your surprised face is not convincing. You look like somebody's great-aunt."

Black and White had both sniffed at him once, and rejected him as both uninteresting and inedible. Only Gray kept watch, following him to the edges of the woods when he left. Her expression was not exactly hostile, but nor was it plumping cushions and offering him hot drinks. The pup began to recognize his smell, and to mew blindly and stagger about when he approached. Ilya would sit, holding the pup in one hand, and tell Feo about the other soldiers in the barracks, about the tsar's twitchy anxiety, about riots in the countryside. Feo rarely heard about the world beyond her own woods, and she listened hard. Again and again she asked him to tell her about Rakov.

"On Sunday he made some of the junior officers hang by their hands from the balcony all night. He said if they let go, he'd shoot them before they hit the ground. I think he's mad. Or maybe just *going* mad. The others say it wasn't like that five years ago."

"Why doesn't the tsar stop him?"

"The tsar has a sick baby boy, so he ignores the rest of Russia."

"I didn't know he had a son!"

"Of course he does. You don't get much news around here, do you?"

Feo stuck out her tongue. "Russia is quite a big thing to ignore."

"Yes. It means Rakov can do whatever he wants. Which would be all right, I suppose, except the things he wants are bloody. He drowned an old beggar in the snow once. The tsar never found out." As he spoke, Feo did her best impression of somebody who was not afraid.

"Hm," she said. "I see."

He told her about the small officers' library, too, from which he sometimes stole books. "They're the only good thing about the whole place. I sleep with a dictionary under my pillow, sometimes. Just to remind me that there are more words in the world than 'Come here, boy.'"

In return, Feo told him about wolf wilding, and their traditions. "We don't give them human names," she explained. "Wolves have their own names: They don't need ours. So we call them by color, or descriptions—like Tenderfoot."

"What will you call the pup?"

"Nothing, yet. Their fur changes color for the first few years, so we don't call them anything until we're sure." Her family had been wolf wilders for generations, she told him, since Peter the Great. He was only pretending, she thought, not to be impressed.

Ilya was there the day Tenderfoot first learned to tear open her own meat, and watched, from a safe distance, as Feo and the wolves rolled together in the snow in triumph. He helped coax Tenderfoot into a run, pushing from behind, while Feo flew ahead on skis, calling encouragements in Russian and in her best Wolf. He was there the day Tenderfoot discovered the frozen elk and crunched it up, victorious, bones and all, only to vomit extravagantly over Ilya's boots.

"That's not going to be easy to explain," he said, as Tenderfoot retreated, looking smug. "Rakov beats you if your boots and buttons aren't polished."

"Here." Feo passed him a rag. "Wipe them off. Use the snow as polish."

"They'll still smell."

"So say it's a fashionable perfume in Saint Petersburg. Anyway, you can't live with animals and care about a bit of dirt."

"Well, yes. Anyone looking at you would reach that conclusion. But I think most people would agree that vomit and dirt fall into different categories of disgusting."

Feo stuck out her tongue. White, suspecting food, did likewise. "Don't talk like a grown-up at me. I meant, most people think they like animals, but they only like the *idea* of them. Real animals mean real dirt."

"Feo, my socks have chunks of elk in them!"

"It's nice! It means she trusts you!"

The day the pup opened his eyes they had a feast. They hid behind the house, out of sight of possible soldiers, and built a snow throne for the pup and put a red cushion on it, stolen from Marina's bedroom. His teeth had yet to grow, but he spent the whole feast trying to tear the feathers out of it with his gums. Food was always plain by the tail end of winter, and so when Ilya pulled a pie from his pack, Feo felt her tongue prickle. It was mince in a red sauce, which ran over their hands and dyed the snow blood colored.

"Where did you get this?" asked Feo. It tasted boldly of tomatoes and spices. The pastry was flaky and full of butter, better than any she had ever tasted.

"I stole it! It was easier than I thought it would be. I mean, I expected to feel worse."

A raven flapped by. Feo pointed at it, and then to Tenderfoot. "Get him, Tenderfoot!" The wolf licked her pup and stayed where she was.

"You see that face," said Ilya. "She's humoring you. That's the face people make when you tell them you're planning to crochet a ball gown for your cat, or paint your sheep orange."

"Shut up," said Feo. "She's getting faster every day. I know what I'm doing."

"You shut up," said Ilya, "or I'll tell General Rakov about Tenderfoot."

Feo ignored him. He would, she knew, sooner swallow his own tongue than turn in the wolf and her pup. "Mama says wilding is helping a wolf work out that she was born to be brave. That's a difficult thing. I don't need help."

This was one of the things Feo turned out to be wrong about: Ilya's help saved her life.

It was deep into the night when he knocked on her window. She had been dreaming of the pie, and waking felt an injustice. She hauled open the window, wincing at the night air.

"What do you want?"

Ilya didn't answer. He was making little retching sounds, like a sick cat.

"Ilya! What's wrong?"

"I . . . skied . . . fast," he panted.

"Why?"

"Warning you. They're coming. General Rakov. Four others."

The air in front of her eyes turned suddenly muddy. "Are you all right? Quick, come inside!" She grabbed him and tugged him up over the windowsill, not noticing he was still strapped to his skis. He thrashed, and then he was in. There were wet streaks on his face.

"What's happened?"

He spoke so quickly she missed it the first time and had to make him repeat it. "Tenderfoot killed a cow. And food's been going missing. They said she stole a pie."

"But you stole that pie! For us!" Feo stared at him. Then she shouted, "Mama! *Mama!*"

"And when they went after her, she bit a soldier. They shot her."

"Shot her?" Feo stopped moving. The world stopped with her.

"I'm so sorry. I tried—"

"But—Tenderfoot? They shot Tenderfoot?" Feo dropped his ski pole.

"Yes. She's dead."

"No." It came out creakily, not her voice at all.

"Feo—"

"She was alive four hours ago. I gave her half a jackdaw." Feo sank down against the wall. "Are you sure?"

"I'm sorry, Feo."

"They can't have. Ilya, they couldn't have." Tears were dripping down her chin into her hair.

"They did. She's dead. I tried! I swear, I tried. I couldn't stop them." She saw for the first time that teardrops had frozen on his nose and chin.

Feo felt the ground sway under her as she sat on it. "Who? Tell me who. I'll kill them!"

"There's no time for that—they're coming to shoot all the others. They're going to arrest your mother. For defiance of the tsar."

"The tsar? How can you defy someone you've never met?"

"They say she ignored the warning. Please—" Ilya took hold of both her arms and tried to pull her to standing. *"Feo!"* His nose was running, snot lapping down over his lip, and his face was wet. "They're coming *now*."

"When, in minutes, exactly?" Marina was standing in the doorway.

"Mama," said Feo, "Tenderfoot—"

"I heard. It's all right, my love; don't panic." Her mother's voice was sharp, but her presence in the room made it immediately easier to breathe. She turned to look at Ilya. "How long do we have?"

"I skied as fast as I could, but they'll come on horses. Or on the sled. It's—I don't know—half an hour. I'm not good at times. Maybe only ten minutes."

"Thank you." Marina crouched in front of her daughter

and pulled her into a too-tight hug. "You remember the plan?"

"My bag's by the back door." Feo hadn't thought she would need it. She tried to remember what she had put in it. *I should have taken it more seriously*, she thought. It had seemed so impossible that anything would ever change. Home had felt eternal.

"Ilya, stand guard, please," said Marina. "Shout if you see them coming."

"Yes, ma'am!" Ilya saluted, and left them to stand where he could see the road up toward the house.

"Feo, get dressed. You're going to run to the chapel. Wait for me there. I'll hold them here long enough for you to gather the wolves, and then I'll follow. We'll head south, and then down toward Moscow. You remember?"

"Yes." Feo scrubbed her face with her hair. "Of course."

"Quickly, then, my darling!"

Feo's fingers fumbled as she tugged on her thickest skirt and warmest boots. She took a shirt from her mother's room and pulled it on. It was big, but a thicker wool than any of hers. She added her knit sweater, her red cloak.

There was a scream from the door: Ilya's voice. The door slammed open. The house was in darkness. Feo ran out of her room into the hall. There were roars, sounds of breaking and heavy boots.

Four lit torches, four soldiers. Their faces were in shadow, but they were huge—middle-aged men with tough skin—and they carried guns. One barked an order and the others began smashing lamps and windows with the butt ends of their rifles. Feo pressed herself against the wall, her heart bellowing in her chest. She ran back to her room and grabbed a ski.

She heard running, her mother's voice in the sitting room, and then a roar of pain: male pain.

Feo gripped the ski and charged down the hall into the sitting room. She could see her mother's silhouette, backed against the wall, swinging with her knife.

Feo swung her ski blindly. The room was in half darkness, but the man who lunged toward her had the hands and tobacco smell of Rakov. She swung again, turning a full circle and stumbling in the dark. Rakov let out a snort, which might have been anger but sounded like laughter.

"Don't . . . laugh!" Feo rolled her lips back from her teeth. She flipped the ski in her hands, held it pointed end first, and instead of swinging, this time she jerked forward and jabbed.

It worked a lot better. Feo was horrified by how much better it worked. The ski smacked into a soldier's neck, and he yelled and tried to grab the ski from her with one hand as the other clutched at his bruised throat. She tugged it away and jabbed again at Rakov. A horrible yielding feeling told her it had hit a soft target. He roared, and his spit flew in her face as he grabbed at her.

"*No*," she gasped. She couldn't look up; she dropped the ski and ran, tipping over the chair with her knee and slamming the back door, snatching up her bag as she went. She heard a coughing, choking roar coming after her, and then her mother's voice shouting, and a shriek. She couldn't tell who it came from, and tears were blinding her, and something else: smoke. Flames were licking at the wooden windowsills from the inside, and smoke was coursing out into the cold.

Feo stared for several seconds before she understood: Her home was burning. She put her hands over her ears and screamed. Wolf wilders are not supposed to scream, but at the sight of the fire, rage and fear took over her throat. From inside the burning house came a voice, a cry: "Feo! Run!"

Feo ran faster than she ever had before, shoulders forward, lifting her feet high in the snow. A stitch clamped down on her side, and she stumbled onto her knees and dragged herself up again, spitting snow. Her breath tasted of tin and bile, and she felt much too small. And then three shadows came tearing out of the woods and the wolves were there, galloping, panting, and sniffing the ash in the air. She opened her arms, and they charged at her and swept her backward.

"Black!" She threw both arms around his neck and buried her face in his side. But his dark fur against the snow reminded her of something terrible and she halted. "The pup!"

The side wall of the house roared with flame. Ash flew up into the night air.

"He's still outside the front door!"

Feo ran, half crouching, one hand on Black's neck. The pup was sleeping ten feet from the door, deaf to the noise of fire and men. He was making tiny bubbles of wolf snot as he snored. Feo snatched him up by the scruff and thrust him down the front of her shirt. He mewed, and his claws raked in panic against her stomach.

She was staring out into the darkness, fighting to stop the shaking in her hands, when the door burst open. Black darted around the side of the house, dragging Feo by the wrist, his teeth puncturing her skin. As they passed, one of the windows exploded outward; fire licked at Feo's cloak. The roof sparked and shuddered. And then human voices. Feo froze.

Soldiers were backing out of the house, coughing and wiping their faces. And with them someone else: Feo's heart pitched.

It was her mother, silhouetted against the burning house. Her shoulders were pulled backward by her hands, bound behind her back, and her eyes and mouth wrapped in strips of sacking. A soldier walked on either side of her, hands on Mama's arms.

Feo bit down on her own wrist to stop herself from screaming. Mama stumbled, slipping blindly in the ice, and the soldiers heaved her roughly to her feet.

Feo heard a snort: It came from the doorway. Rakov stood inches from the tongues of flame coming from the house. One fist was pressed into his eye and one sleeve was covered in blood, and his chest was heaving in laughter. It was uneven laughter: phlegmy, ragged, rising staccato into the night. It was the kind of laughter that makes you doubt the things you thought you knew about the world.

Feo braced herself against the wall, her breath stumbling. She pinched her eyelids to wake herself up. When that didn't work, she grabbed a fistful of snow, rubbed it into her open eyes, gasping at the pain. She had to be asleep: These things did not happen.

They kept happening.

Rakov beckoned the third soldier to help him onto his horse. His laughter had passed, and he scooped up a ball of snow and pressed it against his eye, his face managerial.

"Check around the woods to the west. The girl will probably be with neighbors. Burn their houses if necessary."

The soldier hesitated, swallowed, nodded.

"Look for the boy, too—the feeble one. Bring him back to me for disciplining. And *this*." Rakov jabbed a finger at his eye, at the blood drying in the wrinkles in his cheek. "If I hear the officers gossiping about this—about the girl—it will be you, Davydov, who I will come to for an explanation." The firelight illumined Rakov's face, and his mouth spasmed, up and to the side.

"Sir." The soldier wiped soot and sweat from his face and saluted. His hand shook on the way down.

Feo's dinner rose up in her throat. Suddenly Black was butting the backs of her knees. Bewildered now, she slung one aching leg over his back. Before she could find her balance, the wolf was streaking across the snow away from the house, away from Mama.

"Wait!" Feo mumbled. "I have to go back!"

But she made no move to stop the wolf. Her breath scraped like a knifepoint against her insides. She felt the world becoming suddenly bendable and misty; fuzziness swept in through her ears and the world swept from fiery chaos into blackness.

SIX

Feo woke in the gray light of predawn, in a cluster of wolves, wondering why it felt as if someone had died. Then she remembered the night before, saw the soot clinging to her skin, and her arms and legs began to shake.

"Mama!" she whispered.

The wolves felt her move—felt, perhaps, the fear in the shiver of her skin. They leaped at her, and for a few minutes she lay in the snow and let herself be smothered in a ball of ruffled fur and wolf licks and accidental scrapes from claws. The pup tried to crawl into her ear. She closed her eyes and counted to ten, and prepared her fists and knees and heart to fight the world.

When she sat up, the shivering had passed, and she saw Ilya leaning against a tree, a sack on his back, a wary expression on his face.

"You!" Feo jumped to her feet. "Ilya! How did you find me?" That sounded accusatory, so she stumbled forward in an awkward hug. He winced, and stood stiffly with his arms by his sides until she let go.

"I followed the wolf prints," said Ilya. "Your mother told me weeks ago what to do if anything went wrong." He wore Marina's green cloak. "She said I should take it, while you were dressing," he said, seeing Feo's face, "to cover my uniform."

"The plan didn't work," said Feo. "It broke."

"No," he said heavily. "I know. I saw."

"Mama swore it would be all right! We were going to run—"

"It would have worked, I think. I think she would have got away if they hadn't set fire to . . ." He seemed not to want to say "your home." He grimaced. "It was the fire, Feo. It blocked her way out."

"Is the whole house gone?" Feo tried to sound offhand. She tried not to think of the stars she had painted on the ceiling, or the marks that generations of wolves had made on the door. She failed on both counts.

He nodded. "You should go. There's no point waiting here; they'll come back for you."

"For me?"

"Yes, you. Because of what you did to Rakov."

Feo tried to make her voice sound innocent. "What about him?" It didn't work. The vowel sounds were those of a person who has shed blood. "It wasn't deliberate! Or, at least, not totally deliberate."

"I went back, to bury Tenderfoot, before I came here. The sergeants were whispering. They're saying you're some kind of witch child."

"Because I hit someone with a ski? Witches don't use skis!"

Ilya shrugged. "Rakov's looking for you. He's angry. And embarrassed. I think that's even more dangerous than angry."

"I've got the wolves. I'm not afraid of that," lied Feo.

"You are, Feo! Or you should be!"

Feo made her best hideous face at him: She stretched her tongue to touch her nose and turned her eyelids inside out. It made her feel very slightly better, although the pup did try to bite her tongue.

"None of this should have happened," she said. "All we wanted was our own lives: nothing else. Just the wolves, and the snow, and Mama. And books, and hot blackberry mulch to drink. We were happy, just us." Her body gave another great shiver, and she sat down among the wolves.

Ilya pulled at her, tugging under her armpits. "Get up! You haven't seen what Rakov does to people. The other boys say if you cut Rakov, he bleeds snow."

"No, he doesn't. I saw." She tried to smile.

"You're not taking this seriously! Look, he's . . . he wakes up in the night sometimes and orders us boys to light the fires—there are twenty-four of them—or he'll set us alight."

Feo tried to shrug.

"And then he orders the oldest of the soldiers, the ones with no teeth and arthritis, to fight each other—to the *death*, Feo. And the other men put bets on the winner."

Feo laid a hand on Black's head for comfort.

"And he barricades people inside their houses and sets fire to them. He wanted you to burn to death."

"Well, everyone has to learn to live with disappointment." Her smile was stiff as rock now.

"Feo, this isn't a joke."

Feo stopped smiling: It had been a grim one, anyway, not worth keeping. "I know that! They have my *mother*!"

"That's what I'm saying!" Ilya tugged at her sleeve. "That's why you need to go."

"I know," said Feo. She wiped the ice from her eyebrows

and jumped up and down. Some of the fuzziness in her head cleared. "I'm ready now."

"So . . . which way are you going?"

"I don't *know*!" said Feo. "That's the point! I don't know how we're going to find her. I don't even know where they've taken her!"

Ilya was staring. "What? Yes, you do!"

"I don't! They didn't give me a map!"

"But you must know! They've taken her to Kresty Prison, in Saint Petersburg, to stand trial."

"Trial for what?"

He looked uncomfortable. "You heard what General Rakov said. He said she was in defiance of the tsar. That's treason, technically. Your mother will be sent to a camp."

"Camping?" Feo drew her eyebrows together. Camping was not something you did in the winter, unless you enjoyed watching your toes shrivel up and fall off.

"A labor camp." Ilya was turning red. "You know. In Siberia. Like the tsar has."

"I don't think she'd want that."

"No," said Ilya. He looked at her oddly. "No. But she'll be held in prison first, before trial."

"How long for?"

"They can't try her before Friday; that's when the judge

comes down from the Transcaspian Oblast. Today's Saturday."

Feo bit her lip. Six days. "And the prison? You know where it is?"

"Everyone does! It's guarded by imperial soldiers like me. I mean, not exactly like me. Bigger."

"Then it's easy! I'll go and get her!" A trickle of warmth ran through Feo's insides. "And you know the way?"

"Of course I do."

"So you could get us there!"

"I . . . I *could*. But . . . nobody ever said anything about me coming. . . ."

"You're scared!"

She expected him to deny it: Any normal person would. But he nodded, as matter of fact as the weather. "Of course I'm scared. I know Rakov."

"So you're not coming with me?"

"I didn't say that. I just . . . Do you *want* me to come?"

"What?" It should have been obvious. Feo glared around the snow. *Wolves are much easier to understand than people,* she thought. Wolves, and stars, and snow: Those things made sense. "Yes, of course, you idiot!" She realized it was still not coming out as friendly as she'd hoped. She tried again.

"Please. Do come." Her eyes refused to meet his, so she spoke to his gold buttons. "I don't want it to be just me.

I've got the wolves, but I'd like . . . someone who speaks Russian." Someone, she didn't say, with a kind of bravery she'd not encountered before. A softer, unobtrusive, halting kind.

"But it sounded like you were angry at me."

"No! Not angry. Just . . . scared." Feo firmly believed that if ever you told someone you were scared, sooner or later you'd have to kill him. But Ilya was different.

"Then I'll come. Obviously."

"Ypa!" Feo clapped her hands, and he lunged sideways.

"Please don't hug me again, if that's what you're planning! You hug hard."

"Quick, then!" Feo covered her blush by turning to gesture at the woods. "Which way? Let's go!"

He stared around at the snow. "Well, but . . . I only know when we get *inside* Saint Petersburg."

Feo stared at him. Truly, she thought, boys were not as good as wolves.

He said, "We could ask for directions. If we see anyone."

"No, we can't! Don't you *dare*! We can't draw attention to ourselves now. And wolves are quite attention seeking."

"But," he said, "Saint Petersburg is due north from Rakov's outpost; and we're close to there now. Except, we don't know which way is north."

Feo laughed: The warmth came flooding back. "Yes, we do! With a compass!"

"I don't have a compass. Do you?"

"We can make one. At least, I can. Mama showed me once. Quick!"

She took one of the pins out of the bottom of her cloak. "Do you have a can or a cup?"

"I've got a bowl. A wooden one."

"That's perfect. And I need some water."

Ilya looked around. "Where from?"

"The snow, Ilya!"

He looked helplessly around him. "How do I make it into water?"

"Warm it in your mouth, silly. Like this." She pushed a lump of snow the size of the wolf pup into her mouth, pushing down on the bridge of her nose to stop the cold from shooting to her head.

Ilya copied her, packing his cheeks, then choked and spat out the ice, clutching at the sides of his head. "My *brain*!"

Despite everything, Feo grinned. "I'll do the water if you can find us a piece of bark. Here, take my knife."

Feo unplaited her hair. Her hands felt warmer: Hope, she knew, can control body temperature as much as weather. She rubbed the pin, bottom to top, bottom to top, counting under her breath. Fifty, Mama had said. She pictured herself and the wolves bursting into the jail, her mother's arms sweeping her up. Her hands moved faster.

Ilya came running through the woods carrying a lump of bark carefully in both hands, as if it might escape. Feo sliced off a piece the size of a postage stamp and slid the needle through it. She dropped the needle and bark into the bowl. It spun in the water—first clockwise, than counterclockwise; then it came to a halt.

"There!" said Feo. "The sharp end points north. Saint Petersburg, Ilya! Let's go. Do you know, I've never even *smelled* a city."

"Would it be best to take it in turns on my skis? Or one ski each?"

"No. I don't know if he'll let me—but if he will, I'm going to ride Black."

"*Ch-yort!*" There was awe in his voice.

Feo approached Black carefully. It had been one thing, in the blur of last night, to make a wolf into a horse—but a very different thing in the sharp light of a winter morning.

How do you ask a wolf if you may ride on his back? She licked her fingers and rubbed the fur behind his ears (she had discovered years ago that actually licking the wolves led to fur balls) and whispered calming words into his ear.

Very slowly, she stretched her leg over Black until she was standing astride his back. She lowered herself to sit. She held her breath and lifted her feet off the ground. Black barely seemed to feel her weight: He twitched his ears and ran a few steps, circling Ilya.

It felt very strange to ride a wolf: not blunt, like a horse, but angular. It was like riding on leather and springs. There was immense power under the skin and fur. She had always known Black was strong, but she had never felt it so vividly.

She leaned over his neck and stroked his nose. Black licked her knuckles.

"I'm going to take that as a yes."

Feo was working out where best to put her feet when she saw that Ilya was hovering awkwardly, apparently trying to attract her attention. To hover in the snow is different from hovering on summer earth—it requires more movement around the feet and knees. Ilya looked like he was line dancing on the spot.

"What is it?"

"Can I ride one of the wolves? We'd be so much faster."

Feo looked at White, at Gray. "I don't know. You *could*, physically. Gray's almost as strong as Black. But I don't know if she'll let you."

"Right." Ilya approached Gray. "Here, wolf. Here, wolfie, wolfie. Nice wolf."

"Don't do that!" said Feo sharply.

"What?"

"If you talk to her like she's an idiot, she'll definitely eat you. Just hold out your hand, and if she doesn't snap it, you could try touching her back."

Gray, always the most snappish of the wolves, watched with stern eyes. She ignored the outstretched hand; but, equally, when Ilya swung his leg with surprising grace over her back, she did not flinch. Instead, she took off, barely giving time for Ilya to snatch up his skis under one arm. They heard a whoop and then a yelp and the sound of a snowy branch hitting an unprepared face.

Feo grinned. She should have told him to duck. She leaned, wobbling, across Black's head to kiss White's nose. She settled the pup between her legs and pointed out north to her best friend. "That way, *cherniy*, toward Mama."

To the three men in gray coats and golden buttons just cresting the hill, the pantomime was a strange one. The speck of green merged with the gray, and the black with the flash of red, as they shot off toward the north.

SEVEN

They wove through the forest for half an hour before they came out onto a road heading north. It was thin and winding, flanked either side by trees arching above their heads. Their branches sparkled with frost.

"If I wasn't so sure that they'll shoot me if they catch me," said Ilya, "this would be very beautiful." His tone was unnaturally bright.

Feo was about to tell him to keep his voice down, but as she turned she caught sight of his face. It was bluish, except his eyes, which were rimmed with the pink of sleeplessness. Already his lips were chapping in the wind, but he hadn't once complained. She forced a wide smile. "Don't worry. We'll shoot them first."

"We don't have a gun."

"You know, meta . . . metaphorically. *Metaphorically*, we'll shoot them first."

"I think I'd prefer to shoot people literally if I'm going to shoot them at all."

Feo made a face at him and checked the compass balanced on Black's head. "Keep an ear out for carts."

The road was deserted, but Feo guided Black close to the edge so they could leap into the ditch if they heard anything coming. The going was much faster here on the road—though the snow came halfway up the wolves' legs—because there were no stones or fallen logs to navigate.

The wolves had been running fast for more than an hour when Feo first heard the noise. "What's that?"

"The wind?"

Feo looked up at the branches overhead. "They're not moving."

The noise came again. Feo let out a hiss of fear, and she bit a chunk of hair to keep her teeth from rattling together: because it was the sound a horse makes when it is anxious. Nobody she knew could afford a horse. Nobody except the Imperial Army.

She looked back, but the road twisted out of view.

"I think he's somewhere near," she whispered.

Black growled. Perhaps her knees had contracted too tightly and she'd hurt him, or perhaps he'd smelled something.

Ilya was chewing on his glove, his eyes wide. "Where?"

"I think behind us," she said. "We need to get off the road." She slid off Black's back. "Into the woods—we'll have to jump the ditch. Come on."

But wolves do not obey orders unless it suits them. Before Feo could catch her, White turned and ran back along the road the way they'd come.

"No! Come back!" shouted Ilya.

Feo didn't bother to shout. She slipped the pup into her pack, lifted her cloak in both hands, and ran. As she rounded the bend in the road, Ilya came alongside, panting hard. "Run . . . slower," he gasped.

Black and Gray followed, running on each side of Feo, their rib cages bumping against her knees.

As she turned the corner Feo halted. Terror swept through her and she stepped back, trying to push the two wolves out of sight, behind her. Her arms closed more tightly around the pup, wriggling in his sack.

Standing in the middle of the road was a sled carved

with the imperial crest. It shone with fresh gold paint, and set under the blue, frost-clad trees, it was as if the world had been dipped in fairy-tale colors. A horse, harnessed in silver and leather, was frantically pawing at the snow, barely held steady by a soldier. The horse's eyes were fixed on White, who stood, growling, her hackles pointing to the sky.

And in the back of the sled, wrapped in blankets, sat General Rakov.

"Wild?" he was saying. "Or one of hers?"

Then he looked up and saw her; and Feo saw his face.

The skin on one side was puckered, swollen yellow and purple and green. A bandage was wrapped over one eye, and he wore a fur hat low over his forehead. His expression, as he recognized Feo, was one of raw surprise. But as she watched, she saw the twist of triumph in the old man's lips.

"The little wolf girl," he said. "I had forgotten you were so small."

And he pulled a pistol from his belt, saluted at Feo, and shot White in the side.

Feo screamed and Ilya dropped to the ground as White stumbled, rolling backward in the snow. But before Feo could move, the wolf was scrabbling to her feet and staggering through the ditch and into the woods, a trail of red behind her.

Panic gave wings to Feo's feet. She bolted, dropping

straight into the ditch. The snow closed up to her neck and she gasped for air, scrabbling for footholds, crawling up the other side and into the woods. She heard Ilya panting, calling her name behind her; she reached back a hand without looking, seized him, and dragged him farther into the woods, beating back low snowy branches with her free fist. Black blurred past her, following White's bloody trail, but Gray followed more slowly, walking backward, her gums and teeth bared to whatever might be following.

Once only, Feo turned: just in time to see Rakov mounted bareback on the black horse, urging it into the ditch. Its hooves scrambled for purchase to mount the bank, and the younger soldier pushed its rump, forcing the horse up and into the woods. Rakov barked an order, and two more shots rang out.

Terror made the world turn broken and disjointed, and Feo saw only the trees ahead of her. She retched. Snow grabbed at her boots, and she concentrated only on running, dragging Ilya by the wrist, dodging around great white humps of bushes and beating the snowy world out of her way. Ilya was saying something—shouting something—but the bellow of terror in her ears blocked out all sound and logic, and all she could do was run.

It was the sight of White, as they caught up with her, that

brought Feo to her senses. The wolf was staggering now, her hind feet dragging, and as Feo reached her, the wolf's legs gave way. Blood had stained her fur pure satin red. Feo had not known, until then, that wolves can moan like humans.

Feo took White's head in her arms and eased the wolf to lie on her side. Black ran on, then stopped too, looking back like an anxious father. Feo shook her head at him. She hunkered down in the snow, and spat, and dug her fists into the stitch at her side. Ilya hovered uneasily, his eyes staring.

"Have we lost him?"

Feo looked back at Gray. Her hackles stood up stiff as an iron railing. "No," she said. "Gray can smell him." She heaved a breath. "This can't be happening."

"But it *is* happening. So what do we do?"

The "we" was generous, Feo thought. It was her, after all, whom Rakov was seeking, her face that had made his eyes light up with such a metallic shine of pleasure.

"White can't run much farther."

Ilya said, "Can one wolf ride another wolf? Could we put White on Black's back?"

You could not, it turned out, make one wolf ride another. Ilya and Feo together tried to heave White to lie crosswise over Black's back: It was the nearest White had ever come to hurting Feo. She snarled and lashed out with her claws, clacking her jaws, and twisted back onto the ground. Black merely looked pained.

Ilya's eyes were wide. "That's a firm negative, I think." He looked behind them, but the trees were too thick to see anything. "Feo, is he going to kill us?"

"We won't let him," said Feo. She tried to sound strong and calm, like Mama. She tried to suppress the roar of urgency in her blood, to make a plan. "But if White can't run, we'll have to go where they can't follow us. Rakov will be slow on foot, won't he?"

"Well, he's old. I've never seen him run, if that's what you mean."

"In that case, we'll go where a horse can't."

Feo stared around them. The trees looked down at her, calm and waiting. They gave her hope; it was like having an army of her own. This was her terrain, she thought. This was the land she knew.

"There," said Feo. "That way: There's fir trees. They grow close."

She helped White to her feet and they went on, the two children and the three wolves, barely at a jog now, stopping and listening every few steps, navigating into the heart of the wood. Feo kept her hand on White's shoulder, feeling the exhaustion in every step.

The neighing did not begin again until they were into

the roughest and oldest part of the forest, where storms had knocked trees down years before and no woodsman had ventured deep enough to claim them for firewood. One giant oak sagged drunkenly against the other trees, its roots upended. The tree was leafless, but from it grew a curtain of icicles, some as thick as Feo's arm. As they ducked under it, an icicle fell, smashing on the ground, sending Black darting sideways and snuffing angrily. It gave Feo the first nudge of an idea.

"I want to do something here. Will you take the wolves on?"

"No! Your mother would kill me if I left you alone! I'm older than you, remember?"

"Please, I need you to drag the wolves: look, here, by the scruff of their necks. They won't go without being forced. I don't want them here." The wolves turned to her voice as she spoke. Their eyes were full, as they always had been, of fire and nerves and faith in her. "I won't let him hurt them."

"They're *wolves*." He looked at her as if she'd suggested something unreasonable. "Won't they eat me if I try to drag them?"

"I don't think they will. They know you well enough now. Probably."

Ilya licked his lips. "Probably."

"Please, *quickly*. And the pup, too. Here: He's in my sack. There's a hole in that bramble bush—there, at the bottom. If you take them through that, you'll be hard to follow."

He stared, from Feo to the bramble bush, which rose leafless, eight feet tall, sprawling between the trees. "That's a mouse hole."

"No, it's a fox path. It'll be wider than it looks if you beat the snow away, I swear."

She did not wait to watch them go but began digging under the snow for stones. It wasn't easy, and her gloves were soon soaked, but she found four good-size rocks. She dropped them into her hood. Then she ran to a fir tree and heaved herself into its branches, kicking against the trunk for purchase and moving as slowly as she dared, so that the snow would help to block her from view.

This, at least, was familiar: the wood under her hands and feet, the widening view, the scent of ice and pine. She could see bushes shake as Ilya led the wolves in an unsteady parade through the undergrowth—and, in the opposite direction, the movement of branches.

The horse came into sight as if onto a stage. Rakov's face was set, with traces of sweat at his neck and lips. He guided the horse straight for the curtain of icicles.

Feo said a prayer to the saints of good aim and wild ideas. She hurled her stone, not at the horse, but at the oak tree. The first went wide, landing soundlessly in the snow, but the second hit an icicle at its root. It dropped. Rakov reined in his horse and looked up, frowning. She threw another stone, and then another, her aim growing sharper, breathing hard and leaning out from the tree with one arm wrapped around the branch. There was a sudden clattering, glittering cacophony as thirty icicles came loose, showering down on Rakov's fists and lap and horse.

The horse shrieked, a scream of bewildered terror at this sudden torrent of frozen glass. It reared, beating its hooves against the cascade, and Rakov let out a single angry hiss. He grabbed at the horse's mane, but it reared again and he slipped sideways with a great shout and fell. The horse bolted, its mane patterned with broken ice.

Feo did not wait to see if Rakov was moving. She dropped six feet into the snow, rolled, spat out the sludge and what felt like a bit of her own tooth, and ran for the hole in the bramble. She wriggled through on her stomach, scratching her hands, and then straightened up. A grin had taken over her face despite the fear still in the air. Adrenaline kept all pain at bay, and she let out gasps of relief as she sprinted down the trail the wolves' feet had left, brushing aside branches, looking neither back nor to the sides but only at the path laid out for her.

Gray saw her before she saw Gray. The wolf gave a rumble

of recognition, and Feo cannoned straight into her, sliding sideways, and fell down flat on her back. Four faces loomed over hers. The hairless one smiled.

"Did it work?"

Feo sat up. "Better than I expected."

"Is he still coming?"

"I think so. But not yet." She rested her hand on White's nose and counted her breaths. They were shallow but steady. "I think she can carry on. We'll have to be slower, though." She swung her leg over Black's back. "I'll tell you about it later. We'd better keep going."

"Toward Saint Petersburg!" Ilya looked as relieved as she felt. "You'll love it, Feo." He handed her the pup, who wriggled in her arms before settling down to sit on top of Black's head. "It's a beautiful city." Then, suddenly urgent: "Are you all right?"

"Of course!" she said. Or that was what she said inside: But to her astonishment she found herself suddenly shivering too hard to shape the words.

"You've gone green. I think you're in shock. Here!" He fished a handful of candied fruit from the pocket in his trousers. "Eat this."

"I'm fine, really," she muttered. Her teeth were vibrating. She glared at her jaw as best she could. "Tell me about Saint Petersburg. I need to know what it's like." The fruit was dusty and covered in trouser fluff, but sweet. The pulsing in her head eased.

"Well . . . it's huge. And golden. It's a very tall city: It's full of spires." Ilya mounted Gray and tucked up his feet. "And there's a town square as big as a lake."

Black followed. Feo let herself relax into the rhythm of his tread. She reached out and laid one hand on White's back, pulling her close, and the three wolves walked abreast, a wall of fur and teeth and loyalty.

"And the horses wear plumes, like ballerinas. And there are theaters that look like palaces, with ballets every night."

"We don't have ballet out here. Is it . . . It's not a kind of food, is it? That's something else."

"It's *dancing*! It's magical, actually. A kind of slowish magic. Like writing with your feet."

"Have you seen it?"

He grinned but didn't answer. "And the city's got people selling black bread and honey on the streets, freshly toasted. It's *exquisite*."

"Good," said Feo. She didn't know what an "exquisite" might be, but it sounded promising. "Onward, then."

They set off, slower now, dripping blood behind them, but pointing always toward the north.

EIGHT

They were in open country and the sky was turning evening colored when the wind began to howl. White and Black howled with it

"Oh, *chyort!*" Feo whispered.

Ilya tried to sing, swallowed a gallon of wind and stopped.

The wolves did not usually deign to notice the wind, but Feo could feel Black's anxiety twitching through his fur. As they sped across the snow, Feo saw great chunks of it tumble across the ground, forming snowballs as big as her head. The wolves' tails stuck fast to their legs and the fur was flattened against their skulls. White was struggling, blown into zigzags as they ran.

"There's a storm smell, Ilya," she said. "Blind cold."

"Is that . . . bad?"

"It's not good. It's not even in the realm of good." She leaned forward and whispered into Black's fur, "What do we do now?"

The wind gave another howl; it knocked her sideways and slid inside her kneecaps. It felt angry. Feo's body gave a huge, unexpected shiver that made Black flinch under her.

"Stop it!" she shouted.

"I'm not doing anything!" Ilya said.

"Not you! The weather!"

"Oh!"

Together they shouted, "Shut up!"

There were, in Feo's experience, five kinds of cold. There was wind cold, which Feo barely felt. It was fussy and loud and turned your cheeks as red as if you'd been slapped, but couldn't kill you even if it tried. There was snow cold, which plucked at your arms and chapped your lips, but brought real rewards. It was Feo's favorite weather: The snow was soft and good for making snow wolves. There was ice cold, which might take the skin off your palm if you let it, but probably wouldn't if you were careful. Ice cold smelled sharp and knowing. It often came with blue skies and was good for skating. Feo had respect for ice cold. Then there was hard cold, which was when the ice cold got deeper and deeper until at the end of a month you couldn't remember if the summer had ever really existed. Hard cold could be cruel. Birds died in midflight. It was the kind of cold that you booted and kicked your way through.

And there was blind cold. Blind cold smelled of metal and granite. It took all the sense out of your brain and blew the snow into your eyes until they were glued shut and you had to rub spit into them before they would blink. Blind cold was forty degrees below zero. This was the kind of cold that you didn't sit down to think in, unless you wanted to be found dead in the same place in May or June.

Feo had felt blind cold only once. It had been one night in February of last year, and the walls had groaned with it. Feo's mother had wrapped her in six blankets, five around her shoulders and one for her head and neck, and they had stood outside in the cold until Feo was convulsing and gasping for air. Then Marina had lifted her in her arms and carried her back in.

"Did you feel that? The cold?" Marina had said.

"Of course I did, Mama." You could no more ignore blind cold than you could ignore a bear riding a lion. "Why did you do that? It hurt."

"Because I want you to be brave, my love, but not stupid.

When you feel that coming on the air, you run for shelter. You understand? You run even if your legs are so cold you can't feel if they're still attached or not. It would be stupid not to be afraid of the blind cold."

"But fear is for cowards," Feo had said.

"No, Feo! *Cowardice* is for cowards. Fear is for people with brains and eyes and functioning nerve endings."

"But you're always telling me to be brave!"

"Yes. You don't have to do the things fear tells you to do; you just have to lend it an ear, *lapushka*. Don't despise fear. The world is more complicated than that."

But the weather, up until now, had always seemed on her side. This was something new. Ilya let out a cry as Gray was suddenly buffeted toward Black and the two wolves collided.

"This isn't good!" he called.

At least, Feo thought, the soldiers would be in the same weather. "Perhaps it'll kill them," she said aloud. "They're old. Older than us, anyway." The thought was comforting. Mama had always said, "You will never be tougher than you are now. Children are the toughest creatures on the planet. They endure."

The wind blew again, harder, and a snow-covered branch tumbled toward them, scattering the wolves sideways. Feo gripped her knees more tightly to Black's sides.

Ilya called, "We need to stop!"

"There's nowhere *to* stop!" The wind swirled around her tongue and whipped saliva from her mouth. It froze before it met the ground.

"Can't we build a shelter?" he shouted.

Feo's whole face was stinging. "Where?" They were pacing over what would, in summer, be a vast lake, ten feet of ice topped with half a foot of snow. There was nothing to shelter behind: not even a passing elk.

"This is supposed to be what you're good at!"

It is difficult to make a face in a storm: The wind keeps trying to rearrange your eyebrows. Even so, Feo managed it. "Fine! We'll build a shelter! Pile snow—it'll warm us up!" "Warm up" was, she realized, somewhere between extremely optimistic and delusional, but Ilya was starting to look panicked. Feo scrambled off Black, blinded by her flying hair.

"How?" Ilya said something else, too, but it was impossible to hear over the wind. She gestured to him to copy her and began shaping great armfuls of snow into a ball. Together they rolled the ball across the lake, pushing with their backs and knees, using the wind to help propel it. Feo's blood seemed to defrost as she worked, and soon she and Ilya were sweating, running backward and forward with armfuls of powdery snow, piling more and more until the snowball was more a snow hillock.

The wolves watched, apparently unimpressed. Gray stood a little apart, and every so often she sniffed, connoisseur-like, at the rearing wind.

When the snowball was as broad as a woodshed and tall as a smallish giant, the two children crouched down in the lee of it. Feo pushed her back and bottom into the snow mound, and Ilya copied, molding himself a kind of throne. The wind shifted from a roar to a blur. The relief was overwhelming, and for a minute they sat gasping and laughing at each other's frozen faces. They found that if they carved out a dip in the snow wall for their heads, the wind was dimmed enough to talk. Feo fished out the pup and held her palms, very gently, over his ears.

"I don't want him deafened," she said, "but he needs some air."

"There's a lot of it available, certainly," said Ilya.

Feo pulled an apple from her bag and rubbed the ice off it. "Here," she said. "You can have first bite."

They passed the apple back and forth until it was just the core, which Ilya ate in three gulps, like a wolf. Feo was impressed.

"You learn to eat quickly in the army," he said.

The wolves laid their ears against their skulls and tucked their heads into their hind legs. White's sides were heaving. Feo stroked her ear, but the wolf clacked her teeth together and Feo shied away.

Ilya gasped and pressed himself backward into their snow barricade. "Did she just *bite* you?" His eyes were huge.

"No! She just snapped a bit." Feo tried to smile, but it was unusual for White to be so short tempered. "She's a wolf, you know, not a kitten."

"All right, I know."

"She's tired, that's all." Feo pulled up her hood. "We need to get to a wood, where she can sleep."

"Which way, though, to the city?" The compass needle spun uselessly in the wind.

"I think . . . over there." It was very little more than a guess. "I think there'll be trees that way, soon. We can make a fire." The snow was biting at her eyes.

"Won't we . . . ? I mean, don't take this as criticism, but if we get it wrong, won't we die of cold?"

"I don't know! I don't come out in storms like this, Ilya. You're mixing up being a wilder with being insane."

As she spoke the wind dipped a little, and they heard a new sound. Ilya let out a burp of shock, then slapped his hand over his mouth. Feo hid the pup inside her shirt. They stared at each other.

"Is that . . . laughing?" said Ilya.

"Maybe it's the wind." But it wasn't. It came again: guttural. Feo thought of Rakov and his laugh. Was that a soldier's shape in the snow, or a tree?

"Over there! See: The wolves have smelled something!" She edged out from behind their snowball blockade. The wind punched her full in the face.

The three wolves came running as she scrambled to her feet, grouping themselves in front of her, facing into the wind. Ilya ducked behind Feo. Gray rolled back her lips: Snow blew at the wolf's face and coated her canines, and saliva dripped onto the ground, but she stayed like that, her hackles raised.

A figure was struggling through the wind toward them, shouting something they could not hear.

Feo held her knife in both hands in front of her. *This is it*, she thought. *He's come.*

The figure carried something black and limp swinging from one hand. Feo squinted into the wind; it looked like he had an ax in the other. Soldiers, as far as she knew, did not wield axes. And his coat, she saw, seemed to be made of ragged squirrel fur. Squirrel fur is not soldierly.

The relief of it made her want to leap around the field, but instead she shouted across the field, "Who are you?" The wind took her words, so she tried again, roaring, "Who?"

The answer got whipped away by the wind. But the face approaching was a promising one, Feo thought: young and unpanicked. He was grinning, struggling across the field toward them, and despite her ice mustache, Feo gave a quarter of a smile back.

"What do you want?" she called.

"Need help?" he roared back. He was close enough now to see it was a boy: a boy as tall as a man but, as far as she could tell under the snow, barely older than Ilya. He was startling to look at, partly because of the sharpness of his bones, but mostly because, when he lifted his feet from the snow, she saw he wore socks but no shoes.

"Lost?" he shouted. He must have seen the look in Gray's eyes, because he came no closer but stayed five feet away.

"No," Feo shouted. "Cold!"

"Unsurprising!" he roared back, as another rush of snow came flying at their faces. He gestured with the thing in his hand: It was, Feo saw, a jackdaw. "Help?"

"Help," said Ilya fervently, "would be much appreciated."

Feo only nodded, as much as her frozen spine allowed.

The storm, which renders most people unbeautiful, didn't seem to have touched this boy. His hair was dark, sculpted into wildness by the wind.

"Fast, then!" he roared. He came closer and squinted at them. He pointed at Gray, at White. "Dogs?"

Feo shrugged: It was a shrug that you might, if you wanted to, interpret as a nod.

The boy grinned up at the sky. "Quick! Getting worse!"

"We can ride—" began Ilya, but Feo elbowed him in the belly button and he bit his lips shut.

"Yes! Come!" said the young man.

"You, hold on to my coat," said the stranger. He held out the edge of his coat. "Going to run. Pull you. Hurry." A thought seemed to occur to him, and he pointed to his chest. "Alexei Gastevski!"

Even in the wind, even with the cold coiling inside her stomach, Feo had time to note that the boy was surprisingly bossy. She stared around the clearing, the feeling of unrest growing in her chest, but there didn't seem to be any choice.

"Come!" said Alexei. He set off at a lope, running bent half double in the wind. Ilya's face was white and speckled with ice, but his eyes were bright.

Blinded by the wind, Feo ran in the footsteps of the

stranger, the wolves following. Every few moments Gray's nose touched the backs of her knees.

They jogged northwest, as far as she could tell, through a swaying, creaking landscape. After ten minutes Feo's eyes and lungs had turned to ice, and her feet had turned to fire. She was starting to wonder whether death wouldn't be the more comfortable option when, suddenly, dark shapes grew out of the white.

"Rocks?" said Ilya. At least, she thought he did: The sound was torn away on the wind.

"No! Houses!" shouted Alexei.

They weren't, in fact, houses. It was a ring of ex-houses. Seven buildings, set back from the road and with plots marked out for vegetables: all of them burnt hollow, soot mixing with the swirling wind.

At that moment the storm gave a roar and shoved at them from behind, and Ilya stumbled forward onto his knees. Feo hauled him up.

"Careful!" said the stranger. He gave a guilty, noiseless laugh and gestured onward. "Come on! Very close!"

They picked their way through the rubble and snow. There was smashed pottery on the floor and a tin kettle with a foot-shaped dent in it. Black prowled around, growling.

It smelled of destruction, Feo thought, and of hard work undone.

Alexei beckoned them on. Twenty paces away was a stone building not much bigger than a shed. It had one window, and the smoke coming from the chimney looked neat and deliberate.

"Here! See: Stone doesn't burn well. My sister's place." The boy leaned against the wall, under the shelter of the slate roof, panting and grinning. "Go in! What are you waiting for?"

The wolves faced the house. They sniffed suspiciously. Black let out a growl: Alexei's eyes widened, and he stared at Feo. It was not an angry growl, in fact—there was wariness in it, and exhaustion—but, Feo thought, if you didn't know the difference, it might be frightening.

"I'm not sure if there'll be room for all three dogs," said Alexei. "Maybe"—his attempt at nonchalance was not impressive—"leave the angry one outside?"

Feo nodded. Gray, she knew, wouldn't go inside anyway, and neither would Black. Houses reminded him of his early captivity. But White's injury was oozing nastily.

Feo kissed Black and saluted Gray. "White!" she said. "You *have* to come in. That wound needs cleaning."

Black settled himself against the wall of the house and closed his eyes. But Gray paced away, back into the storm, and lay down among the burnt houses, where she could see the road. She set her nose to point north.

"Come on, White!" Feo tugged at White's scruff. "We need shelter!" When White didn't move, Feo picked the wolf up by her armpits and dragged her toward the door. White snarled but did not bite.

Alexei was knocking at the door, and as Feo approached, it was opened by a young woman. She wore a baby on one hip and a hunting rifle on the other.

"Who?" she said to Alexei, nodding at Feo, who still clutched White in her arms. Feo tried to smile charmingly. She suspected it came out more desperate than she'd intended.

"I don't know—I found them sitting inside some kind of snow castle. I liked their faces! Come on, they need to be near the fire."

The woman looked into Feo's eyes, into Ilya's. She sighed. "Come in." She raised an eyebrow as Feo pulled White past her but said nothing. Her face was very like Alexei's, Feo saw—the same beautiful high bones and sharp edges—but older, and it was muted where Alexei's sparked.

Inside was blissfully warm, and the wind, though not silent, was infinitely softer. Feo scraped the snow off her eyelids and looked around.

There was furniture piled in the corners, some of it burnt in patches and smelling of charred wood, but beautifully made. A pot of water hung on an iron hook over the fire. The fireplace itself was big enough to stand up in, and Alexei dropped the jackdaw next to the flames. Feo felt her whole body prickle as it came alive in the heat. It smelled safe in here, and soft.

Alexei grinned at them and pushed them bodily closer to the fire. Ilya began unlacing his boots.

"There!" Alexei said. "Now we can talk properly! It's best not to talk too much in a storm: The snow gets into your throat. Once, my uncle's tonsils froze and snapped off, honest to God."

"Alexei!" said the woman, but she smiled.

Alexei laughed his guttural laugh. "What are your names? This is Sasha, my big sister."

As he spoke a slab of snow flopped off the front of Ilya's uniform and onto the floor. Under it was his jacket in boiled gray wool, the leather strap across the chest, the gold buttons.

Sasha's face went suddenly slack with horror. "Alexei, what have you done?" She fumbled with her gun, struggling to cock it with the baby in her arms.

"What? I've done nothing!" Alexei looked suddenly

younger, and more like a schoolboy. Feo stared, bewildered, from one to the other.

"You brought a soldier home? You brought death home for dinner?"

"No!" said Ilya. "I'm not one of them!" He had been laughing at Alexei, and his laugh was still on his face but frozen into misery.

"Get out. Get away from my child!"

"I wouldn't ever . . . Nobody would. I mean, you've got a *baby*. . . ." He stopped.

"Leave!" said the woman. "I swore I would burn the next soldier I saw."

Ilya kept shaking his head, but before Feo could stop him he had turned and headed for the door. Two tears were skimming down toward his chin.

"No, but *look*!" said Feo, and she ran to him, spun him round to face the woman, and scraped his icy hair back off his forehead so the woman could see the cleverness of his mouth and the goodness in his eyes. "See, look at his face! He *was* training to be a soldier. But now . . ." *Now*, she thought, *he's in the pack.*

"They're not dangerous, Sasha," said Alexei, though he was flushing. "I told them they could come. I said you wouldn't mind."

"My father made me: He said I had to be a cadet or a beggar. He lied, and told them I was fifteen," said Ilya. "I actually wanted to be a—" But then he jibbed, and bit his lips shut.

"No." The woman did not put down the gun. "Alexei, after everything—"

Feo took hold of the woman's elbow with both hands. "Please. A man—General Mikail Rakov—is looking for me. And . . . I need help." She needed someone—someone older, who knew facts about the world and not just guesses—to tell her it would be all right. "Please."

"General Rakov?"

"Yes. He's taken Mama to prison, even though she didn't do anything at all. He's coming for me now." It sounded so melodramatic to say it that she winced and gave an awkward grin. "Probably."

The woman stared at them: a long, sad look. She put down the gun but kept the baby. "Give me your cloaks, then." Feo saw that the dark patches under the woman's eyes reached halfway down her face. "Come on—don't look so worried, I'll give them back. They need drying."

"Thank you!" Ilya's voice clashed with Feo's. "Thank you so much!" They unhooked their cloaks and stood shoulder to shoulder, looking up at the woman.

"Tell me what happened."

"We're going to Saint Petersburg," said Feo, which wasn't exactly an answer. She reminded herself to tell as little as she could. She hoped Ilya would do the same. If not, she might have to tread on him a bit.

Feo went on. "We'll go as soon as the snow calms down." She whispered to Ilya, "Let's stay near the door. Just in case." And louder: "Come, sit here, White."

"*Everyone* should sit," said Alexei. "We've got no chairs, but that's best-quality Russian dirt floor. You're wasting it by standing on it."

Feo sat, and White leaned against her shoulder. Her breath was rough. Feo stroked her, and helped her lie as comfortably as she could on her uninjured side.

"What happened to your dog?" said the woman.

"Rakov," said Feo. "Not the first time, but the second . . . It's quite complicated, but, basically, Rakov happened. What happened here?"

Alexei put his hands in the tips of the flames to warm them. He smiled half a smile. "Rakov happened. Not personally, of course." He swiveled his position and set his elbows near the flames. "He sent a dozen men. They rounded us up. They said we had a choice: We could run or be shot."

"*What?*" said Feo. Ilya only groaned.

"Most people ran to the next village. Sasha couldn't: Her husband's away, and Varvara had a fever. I helped them hide. Our grandfather used to keep horses in here. It was my fault—*sort* of my fault—that they came at all."

"Why?" said Feo, just as Ilya said, "Was anyone hurt?" Ilya edged closer to Feo, and she put her arm around him, shielding the sight of his buttons from the woman and baby.

"Yes, hurt, but nobody was killed this time, except some animals: eleven cats, a horse. They shot the horse, burned the cats."

"*Burned* the cats?" said Feo. She swore, the worst word she could think of.

Ilya nodded. "That makes sense."

Everyone turned to stare at him. "Do you want to . . . elaborate on that statement?" said Sasha.

"They used to say at the camp that he likes fire. He says nothing scares humans more than to see the things they love burn."

"There used to be a store here," said Alexei. "It had a dozen sacks of sugar; when they burned the store, it turned to toffee. It's the only thing that didn't turn to ash, so we've been eating that. You'd be amazed how quickly you get tired of it."

Sasha smiled: Her smile was two parts exhaustion, one part sadness.

"When was it?" asked Feo.

"Two days ago."

There was a long and meaty silence.

"Can I hold the baby?" asked Feo. It seemed a good way to change the subject. She had never met a baby properly. It was surprisingly heavy, and the head lolled around alarmingly, but it was warm to touch. Its hair was soft as wolf fur.

"Hello," she said. "Hello, pup." She rubbed her nose against the baby's. Sasha, watching, flinched a little, but did not move.

The noise that came from the baby was not a howl but a mew—the sounds of a small person deciding whether to cry. It was also, coincidentally, the sound of a newborn wolf pup.

Feo felt the wolf pup jerk into wakefulness inside her shirt. There was a scrabbling—she winced as one of his claws got stuck in her skin—and then the nose of the wolf pup appeared under her chin. The baby mewed again. The pup mewed back.

"This is my other . . . dog," she said, indicating the wet snout.

Sasha looked from her baby to the pup, and back again.

Feo said, "He'll be good, I promise. He's got no teeth yet, so he can't bite. And he won't pee on the baby or anything. Probably."

The pup sniffed the air, making the bubbling noises in his chest that were the closest he could get to growls. Then he caught sight of the baby and gave out three tiny yaps of horror.

Feo laughed. She sat the baby in her lap, propped against her stomach, and scooped up the pup. "It's just a baby, *lapushka*," she said. "A human one. See? Hush, please! We're guests."

She set the pup in front of the baby. They sniffed each other, then the pup licked the baby's bare feet. The baby squealed gleefully. It was the best noise Feo had heard in what felt like a very long time. She bent so her hair fanned over both the babies, and sang to them in a whisper.

Sasha watched, unsmiling but uncomplaining.

"He's quite clean," said Feo. "No ticks or fleas. I would know: He's been living mostly inside my shirt. See? No bites." She lifted her shirt to show them her stomach, bite free. She pointed at the baby. "Is it old enough to eat?" Then she realized how that sounded, and blushed. "To eat food, I mean—not to be eaten!"

"*She*," said the woman. "Her name's Varvara. Yes, she

would be. But I keep her on milk for now. There's not much food around."

There is a look that people get when they have not eaten for a few days, a tightness in the jaw and eyes. Feo knew the look: She had seen it in travelers passing by the house. It is not a look you can forget.

"What do babies eat?" asked Ilya.

"Bread in milk," said Sasha. "Fruit."

"I have some bread!" said Feo. "And some apples. If we roasted them and mushed them up—would that be too rich? For the baby, I mean."

"No," said Sasha. For the first time, she smiled properly. She put her hand to her head, as if dizzy. "That would be good."

"Could we swap you, for some milk? For the pup? Just a teaspoonful?"

"Yes. Yes, I—of course."

"Here, then!" Feo upturned her pack. "Six apples! If we put them straight in your kettle, they could be apple stew. Mama makes it at Easter. There's a tiny bit of cheese, too. Cheese and apples are good together. They taste of summer. And chocolate—that must have been here since the autumn. It might taste a bit sacky."

"You shouldn't, child," said Sasha. But she looked suddenly sweeter, and younger.

"Yes, she should!" said Alexei.

"Yes, exactly—yes, I should!" said Feo. "It's what animals do. They feed the pack."

Ilya was making a face. He knelt and put his mouth too close to Feo's ear and whispered wetly, "We need to save some. You don't know how long it'll be before we next get food."

Feo's face burned hot. It can be inexplicably embarrassing to be caught midgenerosity. "We'll be *fine*." She changed the subject. "Why did the soldiers come? It wasn't anything to do with me, was it?"

"With *you*? No! Why would it be?" Alexei began sharpening a knife, occasionally stabbing it at the apples bubbling in boiling water. "I need it sharp. For next time they come," he said. "They burned my shoes and my books. I tried to stop them: the books, especially. I know they don't like you reading Marx, but I hadn't *finished* it. I'd been told the ending's the best bit. It's inhuman to take your books away before you know the end."

"Why, then? Were they"—she tried to sound as adult as she could—"drunk?"

"Nothing like that, bless you," said Sasha. "It was because our young Alexei is an agitator."

"Really? Are you sure?" Feo had heard of agitators and

seen prints of them. They were like crocodiles, but with longer snouts. "That just seems . . . so unlikely."

"'An agitator is a person who acts against the tsar,'" said Ilya, as if reciting. "They are enemies of the government. I read that somewhere."

"Oh! Like they said about Mama." *That makes me one too*, Feo thought, but she did not say it.

"Yes!" said Alexei. He stabbed at the apples in the pot. "And I'm proud of it! The tsar may not be cruel, but he's stupid, stupid in the heart, which is the worst place to be stupid. I read about it: It's a failure of intelligence, and of governance."

"Governance," said Ilya, nodding wisely. He shifted to sit an inch closer to Alexei. "Not good at all." Alexei thumped him on the back. Ilya turned a red to match Feo's cloak.

"Exactly! We've got to change things." Alexei broke off a bit of cheese and fed a crumb to the baby. "If we can just—"

Sasha laughed and took the cheese off Alexei. "No politics!"

"At home," said Feo, "if Mama has travelers for dinner and they start talking about the tsar, I'm allowed to say 'forfeit!' and get down from the table."

"It matters, though!" said Alexei. "It's not *politics*! It's life!"

"It's more likely to be death," said Sasha. "Stop it, just

for now, Alexei. Remember, you promised to stop once the soldiers came. Have pity on your poor big sister. I'd like you to reach your sixteenth birthday unarrested, please."

Alexei ignored her. He lay back until his hair was almost in the fire and talked about serfs and revolutions and the persecution of the Jews and a man called Marx until Feo's ears buzzed. He talked at twice the pace of anyone Feo had met, and tugged at his hair until it crackled with electricity. He talked over Ilya's interjections, over the baby's giggling in a pile with the pup, and as the storm grew louder he talked harder and faster than the wind. It was dizzying.

Suddenly, abruptly, he stopped, grinning and breathing as if he'd run a race. He sniffed. "Those apples smell done— don't they, Sasha?"

Sasha smiled, shaking her head at him, and reached down some bowls from the mantelpiece.

"Food," he said, "is the only thing more important than justice."

"We ate a big lunch," lied Feo. "We only need a little bit."

The apples were sweet and hot. Sasha produced some slabs of the burnt sugar, and they used them to spoon up the pulp. Feo ate hers too quickly, and spent the next ten minutes picking the peeling skin off the roof of her mouth. She shared out the bread, and she and Ilya made sandwiches with lumps of cheese softened over the fire.

The taste was spectacular after eating nothing but snow.

She shook White awake and held out half her sandwich. White had always loved cheese, and as the wolf chewed, it seemed to give her courage. Cheese often does. White approached Alexei and sniffed his feet. The boy stiffened.

"Does he bite?"

"She. I don't actually know," said Feo honestly. "She's never met so many strangers at one time before." White was not growling; she looked warm and tired. "No. Probably."

White's tongue came out. Alexei gasped as it reached his ankles. Then White began to lick Alexei's toes.

"That tickles!" he said, but he kept his feet still, and the expression on his face was respectful, Feo thought. She grinned at him.

"That blood, there—is she all right?"

"I don't know." Feo chewed on the inside of her mouth. "I think not really, but I'm not sure what to do."

"Do you have bandages?" asked Sasha.

"We don't," said Ilya. "Just our socks."

"No, keep your socks," said Sasha. She was watching from the one chair in the place, balancing the bundle of pup and baby on her lap. The pup held the baby's hand in his jaws and was drooling lovingly. "You'll need them. Socks are key ingredients for adventures."

"How do you know we're—"

"I just do. But you could clean the wound, at least. Alexei, my towel's over there—use that."

Feo's cloak was steaming in front of the fire. The smell, more than the sight of it, sparked an idea. "Would it work if we cut the hem off my cloak? I know bandages aren't supposed to be made of velvet, but it would be better than nothing, wouldn't it?"

Tending to White's bullet wound took the best part of an hour. She lay still while the three of them swabbed ice and bark and dirt from her side. Once or twice the wolf growled, and each time Ilya and Alexei leaped backward, knocking heads. Feo tied the knots: Her hands knew how to read the twitching of the wolf's muscles, when to pull tighter, when to loosen. When they had finished, White's back half was entirely encased in red velvet, and she was much steadier on her feet.

"That looks a good job," said Sasha. "You've got old hands for someone so young."

Feo did not, at that moment, feel very young, but she grinned. The warmth was prodding her brain back to life. "Could we do the same for Alexei? To make him some shoes?"

"Yes!" said Alexei. "Can you?"

Sasha smiled, but shook her head. "They'd need to be waterproof."

Ilya cleared his throat. "Have you got any cooking oil?"

"A few spoonfuls in a jar somewhere, I think," said Sasha. "Most of it burned."

"And soap?"

"I've got a bit," said Alexei. "I can skip washing. Nobody really needs baths in the winter. Why?"

"Well," said Ilya, "if you mix oil and soap and ashes, you get a waterproof mixture." And, in answer to Feo's startled face, "I read a story, once, where the hero makes a cloak out of it. We could coat some strips of velvet with that, and weave them triple thick. It would be better than nothing."

The shoes took even longer than the bandage, partly because Alexei was not good at sitting still while they wrapped the cloth around his feet, but when they had finished, the effect was spectacular. They looked, Feo thought, like enormous blackish-red slippers.

Alexei did a moonlit lap of the house to test them, and came back grinning. "Watertight!" he said. He slapped first Feo and then Ilya on the back. "One point to us, no points to Rakov."

Nobody changed their clothes for bed: Nobody had clothes to change into. Sasha brushed Varvara's tuft of hair, and then Feo's. Feo plaited it, wound it around her head, and held it in place it with her knife, safely in its scabbard.

"Very nice. In Saint Petersburg they would call that statement fashion," said Sasha.

Ilya laughed. "The statement is: This person is probably going to kill you."

The baby cried a little when she was placed in her cot—it was made of a drawer, well nested with furs. Alexei stopped talking about the tsar again for long enough to sing. He sang old Russian peasant songs in a voice that made Feo think of mountains. Ilya listened with his chin on his knees and his eyes screwed tightly closed. He wasn't, as far as Feo could see, breathing.

Feo lay awake, twisting under her blanket, for hours after the snores of the two boys had filled the house. The wind had stopped, and the snow outside looked soft and familiar. She took the thick blanket Sasha had given her, the last of the stewed apples, and a burning branch from the fire. She filled her hood with firewood.

Black was waiting exactly where she had left him; a few meters away Gray lay unmoving, watching the road and the north. Feo piled branches on the ground, lit them with the taper. Black was aloof at first, but once Feo gave him the applesauce and rubbed both wolves down with the blanket, he unbent enough to give her knee a bite and to chew on her hair. Feo rolled herself in the blanket and lay with her face inches from the cinders. Black paced over to her and lay down across her legs: And there is no warmer blanket than a wolf. From her fire a smell rose up: flames burning night air, mixed with frost and the wolves' familiar earthy tang. It was like breathing in hope. Feo lay awake for as long as she could, and it was to the song of the flames and of Black's breath that she at last fell asleep.

NINE

White woke her the next morning. Wolves make very emphatic alarm clocks: Feo had no choice but to sit up before she drowned in wolf spit.

"All right! I'm here. I'm awake." She wiped her eyes and pushed away the wolf's tongue, which was trying to infiltrate her nose.

Alexei stood at a distance, watching. The expression on his face was unfamiliar: full of purpose, and something like respect.

"Here," he said. He handed her a cup of steaming liquid. In his other hand he held the pup, and under his arm an ax. "The white one was scratching at the door. I came out for firewood." He looked down at Gray, at the slant of her shoulders, the yellow of her eyes, and the elegance of her ears.

"That's very much not a dog." And, when she didn't reply, "That's a wolf, isn't it?"

Feo scrambled to her feet. She tried to bluff, to make her voice haughty. "What makes you think that?"

"Ilya accidentally mentioned it. Sasha wasn't happy. She tends to express unhappiness with broken objects, so I came outside. I know who you are now."

Feo busied herself with White, checking the velvet bandage, feeling her nose. She said nothing.

"You *are* the girl Rakov's men are after. I mean, I guessed you might be. But I thought it was just a rumor. I mean, a wolf girl blinding Rakov. You know. It sounds crazy."

"It does sound crazy," said Feo. She held the pup up to her face. He licked her forehead, and she breathed in his sweet, dusty animal smell.

The pup was boisterous after his sleep, and his claws tangled in her hair. "Did Ilya look after him?" she asked.

"Yes; and I woke up before Ilya, so I fed him."

"What did you feed him?" Feo hadn't meant it to sound so sharp.

"Milk and water."

"Oh, that's fine! I mean—thank you." She smiled awkwardly.

He grinned and nodded at her cup, which she had set down in the snow. "Drink it quickly. It's hot, but not delicious. When it stops being hot, it starts being undrinkable."

Feo drank it. It scorched her gums, and she stuffed snow into her cheeks, gasping. "What is it?" she asked, muffled.

"Tea. Sort of. Well, it's the last dust of berries from the summer—dried—and the apple water from last night. And a bit of burnt toffee. And sugar. Ilya found some sugar lumps in his pack. It's got energy in it, if nothing else, and it'll warm you."

"Thank you. It's"—she couldn't say it was nice, when it so manifestly was not—"wet," she said.

He hunkered down beside her in the snow, a safe distance from the still-sleeping wolves.

"So," he said, "I've got a small question."

"All right."

"What were you doing in the middle of a field with a pack of wolves in the worst storm in twelve years?"

"That's more of a medium-size question," said Feo, but she grinned. She hefted the pup closer to her heart and told him: about Tenderfoot, about Rakov and his black patches of madness, about her mother, and about her journey to Kresty Prison.

Alexei was not a good listener: He interrupted, and laughed in unexpected places, and threw a lot of snow in the air when she told him about Rakov's eye, but at last the story got told.

"And who is there besides your mother?" he asked when she had finished. "Is Ilya some kind of relation?"

"*No!* Definitely not. He's just a boy I know." Feo stopped, considered. "He's all right, though. He's good."

"Good."

"He's got skinny wrists, but a muscly brain. He's read a lot of books. But at home it's just us: me and Mama. And the wolves." Feo wished she could explain—that the beauty of the world is itself a kind of company, and they lived in one of the most beautiful spots in the world. "You can make the snow a kind of friend, if you know how."

"Tell me more about your home before they burned it. What was it like?"

Feo gave the pup her forefinger to chew on. "Do you know the feeling when it's raining outside, but you have a fire? And you've got wolves licking your hands and trying to eat the rug. That's what happiness is."

"Yes! I know that feeling. Well, not the wolves, but the rest."

"And Mama and I would roast chestnuts and dip them

in cream. There's a wire net to roast them in so they don't get burned. At least, there was." Feo flinched at the thought, and the pup mewed in protest. "I suppose that's gone now."

"Exactly! They destroyed your home! Doesn't that make you want to fight?"

Feo shrugged. "I'm going to go and get Mama, and we're going to rebuild the house. Somewhere new. We'll make it exactly like it was."

"You'll need help. Kresty Prison isn't a friendly place. I know people who have been in it."

"I have Ilya," she said. "I have wolves."

"Listen, I want to make a bargain with you." He looked much older than fifteen as he said it. "Will you?"

Feo narrowed her eyes. "Depends what it is."

"I need help. People are frightened of the tsar—and even more of Rakov."

"Well . . . if I was going to choose someone to be afraid of, it would be him. Rakov. Have you seen his face? He's not sane."

Alexei nodded, his face serious. "You could use his soul as a skating rink. But that's the point—my parents, and Sasha and her husband, and all my friends—they think there's nothing we can do."

"Isn't that sort of true?"

"Of course not! But there's only one thing that will make them willing to fight back."

Feo gestured at the soot that had turned the snow black in patches. "I would have, thought burning their houses would do that."

"No! It scared them stiff—literally. They all talk like he's some kind of evil spirit, but he's just a man: You hurt him! He's coming after *you*, a twelve-year-old girl! You're barely big enough to touch the top of the door frame, but you nearly killed him! You're proof that he's not invincible!"

"I don't think I nearly killed him." Feo was eager to have accuracy on this point.

"I need stories. Stories like yours. You could shock people into action. Stories can start revolutions."

"I thought that man you were talking about last night . . . Lenny? I thought *he* was going to start your revolution."

"Lenin's in exile. And Lenin doesn't care about Rakov: He only cares about Bolsheviks. I need *you*, Feo."

"I don't have time for revolutions. I have to be in the city by Friday! It's Sunday already."

"No, listen! It would only need a single village-worth of people to begin. Other people would join us." He grinned, a smile that stretched his whole face into something impish and wild, and Feo wrinkled her nose. People should not be allowed to be so beautiful and so mad. One or the other, not both. He said, "We could change the whole world!"

Feo shook her head. The pup began to scrabble at her wrist, hoping to draw milk from her fingertip.

"Feo, ignore the pup for a second. Half my village wants to fight. But the other half wants to wait it out. They say if we do anything—anything at all—Rakov will just get worse." Feo rearranged her sleeve to stop the pup scraping all her wrist skin off. "Listen, Feo—I need your help. You've got to come and tell the village what happened. If a kid like you was ready to fight him, it would make the others ashamed not to. It would make them believe it was possible."

Feo thought about it: It hurt to disappoint him. But: "I can't. I need to get to Mama."

"*Please!* Just come with me to the village. You wouldn't have to say anything. Just . . . prove I wasn't making you up. Because . . . I might have embroidered things, sometimes. But if you were there!"

"But your revolution has nothing to do with me, Alexei! I have to get to Kresty."

Alexei bit his lips and changed tactics. "Then you'll need food. We ate everything you had last night."

"I can hunt—"

"And there are things you don't know, about the city—about the soldiers and the gates."

Feo looked up, her heart dropping. "Are there? What?"

"I'll tell you, *if* you come with me to the village."

"That's blackmail!"

"Bribery." His eyes—huge, thick lashed, grinning—met hers. "There's a difference."

Feo shook her head. "I'm not interested in politics. I just want Mama. And . . . I'm sorry, truly, but I don't think it would work."

"Well, now you're being boring," he said, standing up.

"I'm being honest!"

"That's the thing, though! If you pick the most depressing answer," said Alexei, "you get to say you're 'brutally honest.' But I say it *would* work, and I once punched a bear in the face."

"Are . . . those two things connected?"

"Yes," said Alexei. "I have brutally honest fists. People say we can't do anything about the way the world is; they say it's set in stone. I say it *looks* like stone, but it's mostly paint and cardboard. *Believe* me. I'll help you, if you'll help me."

Feo squinted. "I'm . . . not sure I absolutely understand. I've never punched a bear. I head-butted an eagle once, but that was an accident. But Rakov took Mama—"

"Exactly!" Alexei interrupted. His whole face glittered with purpose. "He kills people, Feo! It's not just about your mother. Don't you want to fight, for *yourself*? For people like my sister—so her baby doesn't grow up to watch *her* world burn? I didn't think you were the kind of person who would want to live on her knees."

Feo looked at his face, stark and vivid and streaked with wolf spit. "If you promise to tell me about the gates and get us food—real food—I'll come."

TEN

Alexei, Ilya, and Feo were in sight of the chimney smoke of the village when a thought occurred to her, and she tipped herself off Black's back.

"Why are we stopping?" asked Alexei. "Come on! We're nearly there."

"Two reasons. First, I thought it might be best if they didn't see us riding. Just in case."

"Just in case what?" said Ilya.

"Well—just in case they have laws against it. Or something."

"Laws against riding wolves on village streets? Is that likely?" But Ilya climbed off Gray's back and stood beside her.

"Just in case," she said again. In fact, just in case it went badly and they had to make an escape, she thought, it was best if people didn't know how fast they could go. It was best to be wary. "Let's leave the wolves here, if they'll stay. I don't want anyone to hurt them." And then, seeing the incredulity in Alexei's face, she added, "Or the other way round."

"You said two reasons," said Ilya.

"I'm hungry. Aren't you? I think I'd feel a lot braver with food. Alexei, did you bring that jackdaw?"

They found a spot where the snow was thin, and Feo tore down some branches for firewood. Ilya struggled with the fire, fumbling with the matches in cold hands. She watched Alexei, ready to bite him if he laughed—if anyone was laughing at Ilya, it would be her—but he only squatted on his haunches and stared at the world around them. She followed his gaze. The sky was the blue of winter palaces. The snow stretched, untouched, for miles, and the half-grown trees dipped like praying polar bears.

"That's a special kind of lovely," said Ilya, looking up as the fire stuttered into life. "Even if we get caught, I'm glad I came."

Feo halved and gutted the jackdaw. They decided not to waste time plucking it: Instead, they sliced the skin off and threw it to the wolves.

"How long do you need to cook jackdaw for?" she asked. "A minute?"

"An hour?" said Ilya.

"Five hours?" said Alexei.

"We'll just have to taste it until it's ready," said Ilya.

"I volunteer to do the tasting," said Alexei.

None of them had ever cooked a jackdaw, but Ilya had read a story in which it had been done on sticks. "Fictional food's not reliable," Alexei objected, but Feo agreed with Ilya. They cut half the bird into slices and held them on sticks in the flickering tips of the flames, and the other half, still in a lump, they placed in the burning heart of the fire.

Feo threw a few scraps to the wolves on the sly.

The meat from the hot center of the flames kept catching fire and having to be blown out.

"I think it's ready," said Ilya. "It looks cooked. It just doesn't look much like meat anymore."

Feo licked a chunk. It was vile on the outside, tasting of charcoal and stray feathers, but inside it only tasted blank. She and Ilya squatted side by side for warmth. Alexei lay on his back on the other side of the fire. Every mouthful took fifty chews. After forty chews Feo's jaws mutinied against her, and she spat it out into the snow.

"I think," said Ilya, "we marginally overdid this one."

The meat from the top of the flames took much longer to cook, and Feo's arm was aching by the time she thought her slice might be done. She pulled it off the stick with her teeth. It oozed a little blood, but it tasted magnificent, like a bolder kind of pigeon. It kicked energy into Feo's heart. It was rich and soft and the juice ran down Feo's chin. She fended Black away before he could lick it off. He was wearing a jackdaw's feather over one eye.

Alexei kicked snow over the fire, and White peed on it, and they went on. Feo and Ilya walked, not quite hand in hand, but close enough that their arms bumped against each other, their ears still full of the resentful growls of the wolves.

"Keep your cloak wrapped tight, Ilya," said Alexei. "Don't let people see your uniform."

Ilya nodded, laughing awkwardly, and wrapped his cloak so tightly around his shoulders that his neck turned blue.

Feo sniffed the air. "It smells all right," she said. "I think I like it."

"It smells of food," said Ilya. "I definitely like it."

The village was tiny: just a few rows of houses with thin roads between them and a square in the center. The square had a fire burning in a stone trough, where a few children were warming their hands. The houses were small, but each had thick white smoke coming out of the chimney. The square was swept almost free of snow; it was paved with slabs of stone. Someone, long ago, had painted them sun yellow and red. The red had faded to pink. They shone out, like a sunrise. It was a cheering sight.

"Yana did that," said Alexei, pointing at the stone. "She's my cousin. My uncle Grigory smacked her for it."

There was a huddle of women, their heads wrapped in scarves, laughing over something in the street. The sun shone through their shawls and cast colored shadows onto the snow. There were men leaning on doors, arguing.

And their beards were quite amazing. Feo had met few men, and none of them had had a beard like these. You could have hidden a family of mice in the smallest; the largest, which bristled down to the man's hip bone, could have sheltered at least two medium-size cats. They had worn hands with chipped nails, and some were missing teeth. They seemed to have intelligent faces, as far as she could see. It was hard to tell under the beards.

Alexei waved at a man with a high-necked blue jacket and muddied trousers. "Uncle Grigory!"

The man approached. "Alexei! It's good to see you alive. We wondered." He looked at the two children next to Alexei, who were trying to look brave and unobtrusive at the same time. Ilya pointed a toe and studied it.

"Who are these?"

Strangers made Feo's tongue slow, so Alexei did the talking and Feo did the staring.

"Uncle Grigory, we need help. Rakov's coming after us."

"What have you done now, idiot boy?"

"Barely anything! But we need somewhere to sleep. Just for a single night. You can help, can't you, Grigory?"

Perhaps because the man was huge, almost twice the height of Feo and three times as wide, his silence felt enormous. Feo stared at him. His face was unreadable, partly because there was so much beard to negotiate, but partly because his eyebrows and nostrils and mouth and forehead—the places humans let emotion leak out—were absolutely still.

When he did speak, it was not encouraging. "These wouldn't be the child felons? Not the half-grown witches who blinded Rakov?"

"That wasn't me," said Ilya. "It was her!"

Feo mouthed, *Thanks a lot.* She redoubled her efforts to look innocent, but she wasn't absolutely sure how it was done.

The man grunted. "You, girl? That doesn't surprise me. You've a face that says there's a knife in your shoe."

"We just wanted to know," Feo whispered, "if you could give us some food."

Grigory turned to Alexei. "Is this another of your schemes?" he said.

Alexei grinned, impervious. "It might be." He grasped Grigory by the elbow. "Listen! She's got Rakov on the back foot—he's frightened of her—and I think she could persuade people to fight."

"She'll do nothing of the kind," said Grigory. He gave her a glare, and Feo ducked to get out of its way. "You see that house?" He gestured to one of the buildings. Its door was swinging drunkenly off its hinges. "That was Alexander's house: a good man. Rakov took him last week. And my Paul before. Have you forgotten, Alexei? We do nothing to make it worse. *Nothing.*"

"Come on, Grigory!" said Alexei. The grin wavered, but stayed in place. "Don't be like that. Feo's barely met another human before; you'll put her off grown-ups for life. Look— if people want to listen, that's their own business."

The older man's eyes were neither kind nor patient. "If we are punished for *your* folly, that is more than your own business."

But a cluster of men had approached, and one leaned forward out of the group. His hair was gray, but his voice was colorful and rich. "Is this the girl? The one who blinded the general? I say we listen to them," he said. "No harm in listening. Alexei's a child, not a wizard. We don't lose control of our brains by listening."

Alexei seemed entirely unconcerned by the growing crowd, by the size of the men, by their hostile eyes, by their beards. Feo and Ilya edged behind him. The eyes followed.

"Thank you, Nikolai," said Alexei. "All I want is for you to listen!"

"I can't take much more of Alexei talking," said Grigory. "My ears tire easily these days."

"But it's different now! Rakov's obsessed! He's not thinking like a general: He's unhinged—or at least unhinging! This is the time!"

The gray-haired man turned and called to a cluster of men down the street. "Call a meeting," he said. "Yvgeny! Alix!"

Grigory sighed. "Call a meeting, then. You!" Grigory pointed at Alexei. "You, come. But no strangers: That's the law. Leave them in the square. And if they do any damage to the village, I hold you responsible."

Adults started coming out of the wooden houses, wiping their hands on their trousers, putting on caps against the cold. Children followed them, staring hard.

The adults, as they passed Feo, glanced first at her red cloak, then at the ice and dirt around the hem of her skirt.

Feo tried to look like filthy clothes were in fashion where she came from. She tried to look taller.

"Come on. Let's sit down." Ilya took her by the hand and they retreated to the oak tree in the middle of the square and sat down against it, blowing on their hands for warmth.

The children gathered in a semicircle. They were all beautifully clean, dressed in thick boiled wool. There were about twenty of them, the oldest at least five years older than her, the youngest only just taller than the snow, with a crop of curls. Feo wanted to touch the curls but kept her hands behind her back. Toddlers, like wolves, are unpredictable.

"Who are you?" said one.

Feo looked at each face in turn. They were not friendly, but nor were they unkind. Wary, mostly.

"Why are they calling a meeting? Is it about you?"

Feo shrugged. "I think so."

"What have you done?" A boy of about eight, with a gap where his two front teeth should be, stared at them. "Have you murdered someone?"

"No!"

"Stolen something?" He looked hopefully at her bag.

"No."

The eldest of the girls stared hard. "Broken the law?"

Feo was about to say, "No!" when she remembered Rakov's swollen, lividly angry face. She shrugged again.

Ilya said, "We just needed to know some things about Saint Petersburg. She's just passing through. We're all just passing through."

"What *all*?" said the boy. "There's two of you."

Feo glared at Ilya. "He's not good with grammar."

Another girl kicked a little snow at them. "So, what do you want?"

"I'm going to find my mother. She was arrested."

"For murder?" said the gap-toothed boy. The hope was sharp in his voice.

"*No!*" said Feo. "I mean—sorry, still no. For nothing. She's done nothing. But—"

"But that doesn't stop people getting arrested," said a blond girl. "We know that. Being innocent isn't any protection."

Feo nodded. "I'm not absolutely . . . not exactly absolutely innocent. The man who took my mother—I damaged him. A bit."

The boy's eyes lit up. "Did you—"

"*No.* I—what's your name?"

"Sergei. And that's my little sister, Clara." He indicated a five-year-old with a wide smile and a runny nose.

"Then, Sergei, I promise to tell you if ever I murder

anyone. But he's angry. Because, I don't know, he thinks it's embarrassing to be hurt by a girl."

The eldest girl squared her shoulders. She was big, with plump knees and strong arms. "That's not clever," she said. "Not clever at all."

Feo grinned at her, trying not to let the shyness in her chest make her smile go odd. Older children always made her shy. Smiling and shyness together were difficult: It made her nostrils hurt.

Another child—a girl younger than Feo and with wide-set eyes—pushed forward.

"What was his name? The man who took your mother?"

"Rakov. General Mikail Rakov."

The hush that fell on the children was sudden, and solemn. They glanced at Sergei and at the eldest of the girls. Mouths pursed and fists clenched.

"Oh," said Sergei. He sounded half proud, but his eyes were miserable. "We know about him. Don't we, Yana?"

"Yes. He took our brother Paul," said the eldest girl, "to be in the army. But Paul didn't want to—he ran away."

Sergei screwed up his face and, under pretense of itching his eyebrows, dug his fists into his eyes.

"What happened?" said Ilya. His voice was flat. He sounded as if he had already guessed.

"He died, didn't he?" said Yana. "Rakov shot him."

"What?" said Feo. "Is that . . . I mean, how is that allowed?"

"I don't know. He did it, though. They tried to take Alexei, too—that's our cousin."

"We've met him," said Feo.

"They tried to take him, but he fought them. He's fast, you see. And he kicked them in the—well, anyway."

"In the *bits*!" said Sergei. "He did!"

Yana nodded. "He went to hide with his sister. She's ten years older, and she'd bite the head off a wolf to protect him."

"Why would Rakov shoot your brother, though? What had he done?"

"Nothing!" said Sergei. "He hadn't even *killed* anyone."

Feo glanced at Yana, who nodded over Sergei's head. "He's right. Paul did nothing: He was just nice, and big, and a bit slow sometimes. I don't know. If you make it random, nobody's safe, are they? So everyone's afraid. Maybe Rakov likes that." Yana seemed to come to a decision. She hiked her skirt higher on her waist. "If you're Rakov's enemy, you're my friend. Even if you are just a kid. Do you need food?" said Yana.

"We do, quite badly. Do you have something we could carry easily? Bread, or cheese?" Some of the children were nodding. One or two of them were smiling, or at least staring unblinkingly in a more friendly way.

"What are the adults deciding, then?"

Feo shook her head. "Alexei wants them to fight."

"Rakov?"

"Yes. But it's not much to do with me—I'm going to do what I'm going to do."

"Are you going to fight?" said Yana. "I would."

"I don't know," said Feo. "It wasn't in the plan. But some of the things Alexei said . . . I'm thinking about it."

It was then, with truly terrible timing, that the pup decided to pee. Wolf urine has a strong smell, and the day was clear and windless. Everyone, like a chorus, sniffed.

Feo groaned. She reached down her top and fished out the ball of damp fur. He was still peeing.

"Ugh!" she said. "Oh, *lapushka*. You could have warned me." Her front was spattered with pee. "Ugh."

Every child, as though in a carefully choreographed ballet, took two steps backward.

"All right, little one," said Feo. She squatted down and held him at arm's length, and when he was finished, she wiped her hands on the snow. The wolf gave a short, sharp howl. It was small and shrill, but unmistakably wolflike.

The children were already staring bug eyed. Now,

suddenly, their stares became thick and cold.

"Is that a wolf?"

"Yes," Feo admitted. "But only a very small amount of one." The watching eyes were very hard. She covered him with her hair and held him close.

"You're that wolf girl!" said someone at the back. "We heard about you. There's money on your head."

"What?" Feo tried to sound calm, but her eyes flicked left and right, looking for an escape route. "Is there?"

"A lot of money. They said you're not to be trusted. You're a witch."

"Who said that?"

"A soldier came through the village yesterday to tell us to look out for her. For *you*. We should hand her in!"

Feo felt sick rising in her throat, but she got slowly to her feet. "Do you want to come closer and say that?"

Ilya scrambled up and stepped in front of her. She was astonished to see the anger in his face. "Yes, they're looking for her! But those soldiers don't just want her. They want the wolves, too. To kill them. Anyone who hands us in is a murderer." He took the pup from Feo and held him out.

The pup was growing daily—when he sat in Ilya's cupped hands, his legs and tail spilled over the sides. He paddled with his paws.

Clara let out a sigh through her nose, and a button of snot flew out and landed on the pup's face. He ate it. Sergei clapped.

Ilya looked from child to child. "Do you want to be on the side of people who believe he's not worth anything?"

There was a very elaborate silence.

Then: "He looks hungry," said Yana. "Does he want some milk? I can get him a cupful."

Ilya glanced at Feo, who nodded. "Milk," he said grandly, "would be gratefully received."

But as he spoke the pup jumped—more like a cat than a wolf—and landed, twisting, in the snow, hissing. As Feo scrabbled to pick him up, she heard screams, and cloaks flicked past her face as the children tore back up the long street to their homes.

"What's going on?"

"Something over there," said Ilya, and then, as what they were running from became clear, he added, "Oh, *chyort*."

At the far end of the road were three horses, and on them three men. They stood, fairy-tale tall, sniffing the air.

Feo ducked behind the tree, scooping up the pup, pouring him down her shirt, trying to muffle his protests. Fear had turned her fingers wet and weak: She unsheathed her knife, dropped it. Ilya stood in full view, his eyes wide.

"Hide!" She reached out, seized his leg, dragged him around the back of the tree trunk.

The men were coming closer. As they edged out of the glare of the sun, Feo saw them more clearly. Their jackets were not gray. They were shabby men with brown cloaks. Their shoes leaked toes.

Ilya let out a sigh of relief that ruffled his fringe. "Requisitioners! Feo, they're not soldiers!"

"What are requisitioners?" Feo stayed firmly behind her tree.

"Servants of soldiers. Rakov sends them through the villages to collect food and animals."

"Who for?"

"For the army."

"That's stealing!" said Feo.

"Well, they don't call it that."

"They should! Otherwise it's lying *and* stealing. So . . . they're not looking for us?"

"I don't see how they could be. They just go from village to village, you know. They're not very important. There's hundreds of them, though. People call them Rakov's locusts. Didn't they ever come to your house?"

"I suppose they were afraid of us. Wolves have that effect on some people."

The horses came at a walk into the square.

"Where are the men?" called one of the riders.

The doors of the houses stayed shut. There was a crunch of slamming bolts.

Then, just as Feo was letting out a great sigh of relief, Yana stepped out of the largest house, holding a cup filled to the brim with milk in both hands. She froze as she saw the men.

"Where's your father, my lovely?" said the rider. He was a broad-shouldered man, with a large mole between his eyebrows.

"At—at the meeting."

"Get him, then, my sweet, won't you?" He leered at Yana, showing teeth colored a variety of different browns. "Tell the men we're working under Rakov's orders. We've got a list, shows what's owed by each village. In your case that's a hundred kilos of grain. Twenty kilos of meat. And I wouldn't say no to a kiss, if you've got one going spare."

Yana backed away. "But we can't," she said. She was looking around, but the main street looked deserted. "We would starve! There are little kids here."

"That is a commonplace excuse." The second man's voice was sharp. He was chewing on tobacco, and he spat it down into the snow, where it lay steaming. "We've heard it before. They will not starve. You will find a way."

The first rider sniffed. "What's that smell?"

Feo held her breath. She held the pup to her damp front.

Yana was icy white now. "What . . . smell?"

"Borscht!" said the rider, slapping his hand on his horse, who whinnied, easily alarmed.

"Ah," said the second. His nostrils stretched. "Good." The men dismounted and pushed past Yana into her house. "Bring us soup. All of it. We'll find out if you hold any back. And vodka."

Yana's voice was shaking. "Or what?"

"You know the law—or we take your eldest boys, my sweet. Get us some soup and get the men, in that order."

Feo's heart was straining against her rib cage in fury. "I've got an idea," she whispered to Ilya. "I need your help."

"Anything," he said. "What?"

She told him.

"It's too risky," he said.

"I can't think of anything else. Can you?"

"No. But I'm not sure—"

"Wait here." Feo handed the pup to Ilya and ran to the nearest of the houses. She beckoned through the window. Two heads poked out of the door.

"Who here has good aim?" she whispered.

"I do," said Sergei. "And Bogdan." He indicated a boy of about ten breathing through a half-blocked nose. He didn't look promising. "And Yana." Sergei looked around, as if expecting to see her pop out from the snow. "She's not here. They haven't taken her, have they?"

"No, Sergei, nothing like that. But I need help. Will you?"

Sergei looked from Feo to Ilya to the pup. "Yes, definitely! Are we murdering someone?"

"Close enough. Come with me." She led them, crouching low, back to the tree. "We need snowballs. And we need to be quick," said Feo. "They're drinking vodka. I don't really know how long that takes." She started packing together snowballs, making them as big as melons.

"Quicker," said Ilya. His hands were fumbling in the snow. "We need to be quicker."

The smaller boys worked fast, but not fast enough. Feo doubled her pace. "They need to hurt," she said. "Pack them tight. Good! That's enough." She gathered the snowballs in her cloak. "Come on." She led the way to the house nearest the horses—a small one with graying bricks—and ducked behind it. Ilya was still making snowballs as he ran. He was whispering instructions to himself under his breath, but when he saw she was looking at him, he attempted a grin. It was lopsided and far more toothy than usual, but it gave her a burst of courage.

"When I shout," she said, "aim for those men's eyes. It's important: eyes and mouth, but especially eyes."

"What's going—" began Sergei, but Ilya put a finger to his lips.

Feo turned to the woods, cupped her hands to her mouth, and howled.

There was a beat of silence. Children's faces appeared at the windows all along the street.

Feo howled again, and from the woods came a reply: Gray's guttural cry, and then Black's. Feo nudged Ilya, and he joined in. His howl was surprisingly excellent.

The requisitioners stumbled out of the house, a jug of spirits slopping in the hand of the tallest. They ran, staggering, toward their horses, struggling to cock their rifles. "Wolves!" one of them roared, and then tripped over his toes and performed a painful-looking split on the ice.

Feo picked up a snowball in each hand. She howled again. The men heaved themselves onto their horses, their feet slipping drunkenly in and out of their stirrups.

And from the woods came the pack of wolves, running low, the fur on their backs rippling as they approached. Her wolves, Feo thought, definitely had a sense of theater.

"Now!" cried Feo. As the men lifted their rifles, the children attacked. Sergei and Bogdan came charging out from behind the house, hurling snowballs at the men's eyes, hands, ears, gun barrels. Sergei's aim was erratic, but Bogdan's was brisk and true.

"Devil take—" roared a requisitioner. "Wol—!" Just as he raised his gun to his eye, Feo's snowball caught him in his open mouth.

Behind them, out of the corner of her eye, Feo saw the meetinghouse door burst open. The requisitioner's rifle rang out and a bullet drove into the snow, meters away from the approaching wolves.

"No!" Feo's heart caught in her chest. "Get them in the eyes! Make sure they can't shoot!" She kept hurling snowballs, showering the men with ice that cut at their faces and knocked them sideways. Feo howled one last time, and Gray leaped, her jaws bared, at a horse's side. Feo hadn't meant her to get so close. She shouted, "Gray, no! Back!"—but even as she did, the horses reared. Screaming in terror, they fled down the main road. The sacks, loosely empty over their saddles, bounced against their sides. The men, hanging blindly on to their horses' necks, disappeared over the horizon.

ELEVEN

Four hours later Feo sat by a roaring fire in the middle of the square, wrapped in eight blankets, ducking the grateful kisses of strangers and chewing a kebab on a wooden stick. The juice of it ran down her wrist, and the pup kept trying to insert himself into her sleeve. Her head was still in a whirl.

Alexei had taken in what had happened faster than anyone. Pushing through the crowd of staring men, he had dragged her into their center and raised her hand above her head like a prizefighter.

"You see?" he had shouted to the men, who stood, staring and bewildered. "*That's* what courage looks like. *That's* why Rakov is afraid of her!"

She had wriggled free as soon as she could, but she was unable to avoid the stream of strangers approaching her, clapping heavy hands on her shoulders, embracing her with rough cheeks and calloused palms, the women stroking her hair and pressing hot meat into her hands.

They had stayed back, though, from the wolves. In the flurry of the requisitioners' departure, a few stones had been thrown at the animals, but Feo had thrown stones at the throwers and her aim had been better, so it had all stopped fairly quickly.

"They're my friends," Feo had said. "They're no more likely to bite than I am." She did not specify exactly how likely that was.

At last, unable to bear the attention, Feo took the wolves, a lantern, and a haunch of beef behind the tree to hide until her head stopped spinning. The meat, at least, did not try to kiss her.

But the space behind the great tree was already occupied.

"Yana!" said Feo. "Sorry, I was just—"

"Hiding? I know," said Yana. She edged away from the wolves. "I thought I'd get out of the way before the dancing starts."

The thought of dancing was so terrible that Feo pushed it away out of sight. She took a bite of meat, and spoke round the edges of it. "What happened with the meeting?" she asked.

Yana shrugged. "Nothing. It was interrupted, wasn't it? They'll decide tomorrow. They'll decide not to fight. They always do. All they do is talk." There was rage in her voice. It was odd, coming from so soft-looking a person. "This isn't the first time Alexei's tried to make them. He's been wanting to fight since he was thirteen. Rakov's never been so bad as this, though. They say he's going mad, did you know?"

"I think he's just plain evil. Those men—they didn't hurt you, did they?"

"No! They just wanted a drink. Though if the grown-ups keep going the way they are right now"—she gestured at the men dancing around the fire, their boots kicking out in the snow—"there won't be any to give them when they come back."

"Come back?"

Yana nodded. Her face, Feo thought, was horribly matter of fact. "What you did was wonderful, Feo, but they'll come back. You don't know what it's like here. Rakov's men— the tsar's army—they always come back for something. Or someone."

The look on Yana's face made Feo's throat burn. She shook it away and turned to stare at the snow, poking at it with a stick. As she poked, the first twitchings of an idea began to flicker.

"But, look—look! See here." She pointed to the prints Black's paws had left in the snow. "Look."

"They're big," said Yana. "Big enough to kill you."

"Exactly! Those men—they won't come back if they see the prints, will they?"

"But the next time it snows they'll be covered," said Yana. "It's not . . . They're lovely prints, but it's not a long-term solution, Feo."

"You could make them again, I think!"

"What?" Sergei peeked from around the tree trunk. "Are you planning to leave the black wolf here? That would be amazing! I'd take good care of it!"

"No!" Feo shook her head so hard that her hair got caught up in her meat. "Black and I go together. That would be like leaving behind my fingers. And, anyway," she added, as Sergei pouted, "he wouldn't stay for long if I left: I can't *make* him do anything."

"So you can't help us."

"Maybe I can. I've got an idea. We'll need wood, thick wood. And knives. Can you get those? And some people to help. And Black, as the model."

The whittling took less time than Feo had expected. Ilya was meticulously careful; Yana was unexpectedly fast with her hands. They hacked the wood into squares with an ax, and then chipped away with kitchen knives until paw shapes began to emerge, very slowly, from the grain.

Every now and then Sergei would yelp, and the snow around him would be flecked with red, but he tried to bite Yana when she suggested he give up on his, so they left him to it.

When they had four lumps of wood carved roughly into something like the shape of wolf paws, Feo took them into her lap and rubbed the edges with the rough sacking of her bag. "To blunt the edges," she explained. "Wolves are smooth."

Sergei watched with his tongue poked out in concentration.

"There. Now we need string. Do you have any?"

"String's valuable round here," said Yana. "But I'll try."

She returned in ten minutes, her expression guilty. "I . . . borrowed it, from Papa's spare boots."

"Thank you. Now—look!" Feo looped the string around her feet, then lashed the wolf paws to the soles of her boots so that the print faced downward. She took the other two in her hands. On all fours she ran a few steps, turned, galloped the other way. She tried to keep her feet close together: Wolves run in a compact line. Behind her, the prints of a wolf cut into the snow.

"You could do it every day! And we'll get Black to mark

the territory. He's an alpha," said Feo. "That way you'll be safe from other wolves."

"How? Mark how?"

"Well . . . ," Feo said. "You know. They pee."

"I don't want them peeing in my room!"

"No, just on trees! And the outside of houses. It has a scent in it. It warns other wolves to keep away."

"Like writing a 'Keep Out' sign?"

"Yes. Peeing is wolf writing."

"Ugh."

"It's an old trick. It's the only trick I taught them. It's what keeps us safe, at home, from the wolves we wild coming back."

Sergei asked, "Does it work for humans too? I mean, if I peed on my sister's bed, would she have to leave?"

Ilya let out a snort of laugher.

"No," said Feo. "I tried, when I was much smaller. I was angry with Mama about something. It *definitely* didn't work." The thought of her mother—who, in response to that incident, had sighed, and then laughed, and swung her bodily into the tin bath—sent up such a spurt of longing that Feo felt the snow sway under her. She forced the longing down.

Grigory's head peered around the tree. "Ah! There you are.

I heard laughing. You're wanted by the fire. Dancing!"

There was music playing outside the meetinghouse.

"It's all for you!" said Clara. She gestured at the fire, at the circle of waiting adults, and the man with a fiddle poised under his chin. "To say thank you! You and the boy are going to do a dance!"

Fresh horror drenched over Feo, far worse than when faced with guns and requisitioners.

"Thank you!" she said. "But I don't dance."

"Oh, come on! *I* dance," said Sergei. He swiveled his hips and windmilled his arms. "See?"

"Wolf wilders don't dance," said Feo. She wrinkled her nose at Clara and smiled. She hoped the fear didn't show in her face. Feo hated dancing. Dancing was unambiguously to do with being watched.

"You'll have to," said Yana. She smiled apologetically. "It's easier just to do it."

"I don't know it."

"Yes, you do! Dance, wolf girl!" said Sergei.

In fact, Feo did know the steps to this music: Everyone did. Mama had taught her as soon as she was old enough to walk—just in case, Marina had said. Everyone should be able to dance one dance.

The woman's part wasn't difficult. You made little doll

gestures with your hands, kept your head and neck still. For men, lots of stamping and head tossing. If you had a skirt, you swished it. Feo sighed and stuck out her elbows, and swished her cloak. Yana clapped politely. The adults murmured contentedly.

Ilya stepped forward and bowed. He was grinning nervously, but there was a spark in his eyes.

"Can we try to do it as quickly as possible?" said Feo. The heat in her face had nothing at all to do with the fire. "I'm not very good at dancing."

"Dance!" cried someone in the crowd. Feo suspected it was Alexei. She glared.

The music rose, quickened, peaked. Ilya leaped upward. Boys do not have skirts to swish—but as Ilya jumped and spun, scissoring his heels in the air, snow flew up around them, and the air seemed to swish for him. He leaped again, higher, and as the wolves paced into the circle to investigate, Ilya crouched and split-leaped high over White's back.

Feo let out a gulping laugh of surprise. White snuffed primly. There was laughter from the adults, but Ilya's face was shining with a white, bright seriousness.

Feo stepped through her part, keeping her head down: two skips, twist the wrists. Ilya was ignoring the steps: He found a spot of ice and began to pirouette, one leg straight out from his waist and snow flying from the sole of his shoe. Clara started counting his turns, but at eleven she got confused and cheered instead. The crowd around them was growing. Ilya jumped like a cat and landed in front of Feo, and crouched, kicking his legs out like a Cossack.

He didn't dance like a soldier, or like a sharp-wristed child who could not light a fire. He danced, Feo thought, like a lost boy found: like a victory parade.

Feo danced herself to a stop. Nobody, she thought, was watching her: So she knelt down by the wolves, one arm round Black's shoulders, staring. Even the wolves seemed more than usually fascinated. The snow had begun to fall again, and the villagers widened their circle to give Ilya space as he threw himself backward—hands landing wrist-deep in snow—and flipped upright to land on the tips of his toes. He did not wobble. The top of his head had gathered a snow cap. The fiddle player quickened his pace again, and Ilya flew in a circle of leaps and spins, snow and sweat flying off his face. Feo hugged Black tighter, and scrunched up her face so nobody would see the pride in her eyes. She whistled through her fingers.

He came to a stop as the music softened, and let his arms fall to his sides.

There was silence. Ilya's shoulders fell a little, and his ears began to glow pink. He looked down at his shoes.

The roar of applause hit them like a solid wave. It was architectural.

Ilya let out a choking, strangled snort of happiness. "I did tell you," he said to Feo, "that I never wanted to be a soldier."

Feo tried many times in the next hours to get Ilya away by himself, so they could be gone. Alexei had stuffed their packs full of cheese, dried sausage, and nuts, but every time they crept away from him, he seized her and towed her to meet another bearded man or cloaked woman.

"The wolf girl! Look at her!" he kept saying. He grinned at her. "Look—see, this is the one who attacked Rakov with a ski! You have *cheese* older than her, Grigory! You're willing to let her be braver than you?"

So it was pitch-black by the time Feo found Ilya by himself, and the panic in her chest was rising.

"We need to sleep, Feo," he said. He was stretched out on a straw-sack mattress on Sergei's floor, looking ostentatiously comfortable. "And it's dark out there. Tomorrow will be soon enough."

"It *won't*, Ilya! We need to go *now*. It's Sunday! The city's still more than a day away! And then we need to find a way to get *in*, and get her *out*."

"Six or seven hours won't make any difference."

"*It will*, Ilya!" Her voice, she could hear, was growing shrill.

Ilya closed his eyes and snored loudly.

Feo shook him. The snoring grew louder, and the eyes scrunched more tightly closed.

Outside the window the fire was still burning, and the laughter was getting louder and wilder. Men were thumping their fists against their chests; women were dancing in the snow. As she watched, Feo felt her chest contract. She had never been around so many strangers in her life.

Alexei dashed past outside, Clara on his shoulders. He slipped and skidded in the snow. Sergei chased him, trying to touch his cloak, sliding in the ice and shrieking with past-bedtime glee.

Feo thought for one second about joining them, and then pressed herself back against the wall. It wasn't time for playing. They were strangers: Everyone, really, was a stranger, even Ilya. Feo tried to fight back the rising panic. It prickled in her stomach, an unfamiliar fear. Even the snow in this place was thinner and trodden flat. It didn't talk, she thought: It was mute snow. Sitting still became too much to bear.

She ducked outside and caught Alexei by the coat as he ran past.

"Lady Wolf!" He snapped his ankles together and saluted, laughing.

"I need help."

"Name it!"

"You said you'd tell me about the gates?"

"Ah! The gates. The gates to the city?" He seemed giddy, fire crazy. "The gates to heaven? Please specify."

"Alexei."

"Sorry. Right, yes." He grinned. "But you've got to admit it's exciting! It's happening!"

"The *gates*, Alexei. To the center of the city. Please. It's important."

"Well, they're guarded. They didn't used to be, but now Rakov has proxy rule over the whole city. He'll have put them on watch for you, I think. And they check the papers of everyone. At least, everyone who looks like they might be trouble. Everyone poor."

"And how do I get past?"

"I don't know."

Feo stared at him. "You said you did!"

"No, I didn't! I said I'd tell you what I knew, that's all."

Feo turned away from him without a word. She didn't glare; this was too serious for glaring.

"No, wait, Feo!" He sounded more sober. "I'm sorry. There's

a castle a day's ride from here. It'll be useful if there's another storm. Once you're there, it's only four hours' walk to the city gates, or two hours on a horse. We can go there tomorrow. We can get the rest of the village to join us. It's a good place to spend the night. It's northwest from here, to the left of the big pine wood as you approach. Nobody lives there: It was burned out in a fire years ago. The tsar thinks it's bad luck, you know, to live in a house that burned down, and so everyone who's fashionable has to believe it too. Ironic, when you think how much his army enjoys setting fire to things." Clara came running, and he scooped her up. "Come and find some shashlik?" he said to Feo, but he didn't wait for the answer, leaping off into the dark with the little girl squealing in his arms.

Feo looked around, her mouth growing dry. Many of the adults had started to sing, to dance erratically. One of them accidentally put a cigar out on the chin of another.

I should never have agreed to come, she thought.

Feo ducked back into the house. She pulled on the freshly laundered shirt Yana had given her in exchange for her wolf-stained one.

Ilya won't help me, she thought, and tipped out Ilya's bag. She pulled out the lantern and the bowl for the compass. *Mama doesn't matter to him. And Alexei only cares about his revolution. And if he won't help me, why should I help him?*

She picked up the pup from his place by the fire and pushed him down her newly clean shirt. He was affronted but made no noise.

I'll just have to find Mama by myself. I work better alone, anyway. I know about alone.

The wolves were standing guard outside, and they, too, made no sound as Feo led them, crouched low, out behind the buildings, away from the great oak tree, and northward into the night.

They'd gone an hour, through scattered trees, the lantern swinging from Feo's wrist, when both Feo and Gray heard the noise that was neither their own breath nor the wolves' paws.

The wolf growled.

"What is it?" Feo breathed.

But it wasn't hard to identify: It was the sound of a horse neighing, and then, just audible, the coughing of a human. Feo held the lantern high, but there were only trees. She spat on her fingers and pinched out the lantern's wick.

"It's probably just a traveler," she whispered to Black. "Or"—as a sudden warm thought came to her—"Ilya's followed after all!" But she dared not call out.

White, next to her, stiffened. She had smelled him.

"Hush, *lapushka*," whispered Feo. She knelt in the snow

to stroke White's head, to quiet her. "We're alone. We're not here to fight. No howling, not now."

It was no good. Feo had never taught the wolves to be silent. White flicked her nose to the moon and howled.

There was an exclamation from the left. Snow-covered branches moved.

Feo's whole body blanched with fear. She stared around. The thicker trees were a hundred meters away; Feo ducked her head low and tugged at the three wolves, urging them to go ahead of her. "Quickly!"

The going was harder as the canopy closed over them and the moonlight grew dimmer. There were fallen trees and bushes with snaking roots. Black, by far the largest, slowed them: The bushes grew too thickly for his bulk to slide between them.

"Head west a little now. We'll be faster like this," Feo whispered. She walked carefully, her hands outstretched to feel for trees. "Come on. We'll find a willow or something: somewhere to hide."

But as she spoke, Gray turned and began to run, head down, back the way they had come.

"Gray, come back!" Feo hissed. The other two wolves sniffed the air, nudged her, and followed. "White? Black? Please?"

Feo scrubbed the frost from her upper lip and stared around. She took the pup out from inside her top and stroked him, more to calm herself than to calm him. Something rustled near her feet, and she jumped so violently that she squeezed him too tight and he mewed loudly in protest.

The something rustled again.

"Black? Gray?" whispered Feo. She looked over her shoulder. The shadows moved. "White?"

She could neither smell nor hear anything, but her skin was prickling with fear. Something nearby was breathing: human or wolf? Feo unsheathed her knife and ran to stand with her back against a tree.

A young soldier came bursting out of the undergrowth, a lantern swinging from one hand, a gun in the other. Feo had time only to let out the first half of a scream before he grabbed her and smashed a hand over her mouth.

The trees parted and out of them rode Rakov, his horse led by another soldier on foot.

"Halt!" Rakov called into the night. "Feo Petrovna!" He pronounced it "Fear."

Feo struggled, kicking at the soldier's ankles.

"My head requisitioner reported having seen you. It seemed profoundly improbable that you would be so stupid. But apparently not."

She tried to bite the soldier's hand, but he slapped her face and she screamed, *"Help!"* Who, though? There was only her.

She stamped hard on the soldier's instep, pulled one hand free and threw her knife into the darkness: It grazed past the foot soldier's shoulder and he swore, both hands on his gun, trying to cock it in the darkness. Rakov sat, unmoving, on his horse. The lamplight shone directly on his smile.

Gray came flying out of the wood. Feo had never seen anything run so fast.

The soldier near Rakov aimed his gun at her head, but the wolf was on him. She rose on her hind legs and tore at his arm. He shrieked and ran, and Rakov's horse reared, its hooves drumming at the air.

Feo screamed and kicked out at the soldier holding her. As she did, Gray leaped at his shoulder and tore at his skin. The man screeched like a drunkard and turned, bleeding, clawing at the wolf with his nails. His face was lit up with rage and pain.

It was like being protected by a myth, by legend and spit.

Feo's legs loosened. She ran stumbling through the dark, heading for the pine trees with low branches, the pup in her arms, looking over her shoulder as she plowed through the snow. She reached the nearest tree and scrambled against the trunk for a foothold, trying to close her ears to the hideous screaming and growling coming from below. Feo hauled herself into the lowest branches and turned to see the second soldier run, stumbling, into the woods.

There were pine needles in her face. Her heart was beating so hard it shook her cloak.

A shot rang out.

"No!" Feo screamed, but it came out as a wordless roar.

There was a growl of pure animal fury, and Black rocketed out of the shadows, followed by White, making straight for Rakov's feet. His horse let out a shriek, and Feo twisted in the tree to see him jerk sideways, away from the wolf, his gun dropping into the snow. The horse kicked and turned to gallop through the trees, tearing through the branches and whinnying in terror, the rider pressed flat against its back.

She had expected White and Black to chase him, to kill him, but they stood, their noses touching Gray's fur.

For one terrible moment Feo thought they were biting her. Then she saw they were licking a wound in Gray's side, and she let out a cry, higher and louder than the last. Snow fell from the tree into her face and mouth. The wolf was not moving.

"*No!*" Feo dropped to the ground, landed in shin-deep snow. "I'm coming!"

She ran, tripping on roots under the snow, toward her trio of wolves, then stumbled to a halt, digging her fists into her eyes. Her mother's favorite wolf lay on her side, her body on top of the pistol. There was blood in her breath.

"Where are you hurt?" Feo crouched, laid a hand on Gray's muzzle. The blood was spreading through the snow, still running from the wolf's stomach. Feo whispered, "*No. No, no, no, no.*"

The wolf's eyes opened, rested on the girl's face, closed again.

"I'm so sorry—I . . . What've I done?" Feo thought of Ilya sleeping by the fire, of Alexei's ax, of the safety of the vast bonfire. The pup nuzzled at Feo's hands: Feo brushed him away.

"I'll get a—I'll make you a bandage. Like we did for White. It'll make it better." Feo fumbled for the hem of her cloak to tear off a strip of cloth. "Think of Mama, yes? Think of how happy she'll be to see you when we find her." Tears were casting the moonlit night into a blur. Feo's chest heaved, and she struggled to rip the material. "Please, please stay with me," she whispered. "Don't— don't go."

The wolf's breath was more audible now: It sounded thick and wet.

"I think"—a gasp, and she controlled her voice—"I think this will help."

Feo tried to wrap the bandage around the wolf's wound, but it was so dark and so cold. She had never known snow so cold. Gray shied away from the bandage and shivered. Feo had never seen a wolf shiver.

She untied her cloak from under her neck and draped it over Gray's flanks.

The wolf gave a growl of pain.

It was like watching a forest burn, like watching an army fall.

Feo lay down beside the she-wolf, slipping in the ice and snow. Gray's side barely moved as she drew slow breaths, but she moved her muzzle to rest against Feo's chin. Feo touched her nose on the wolf's nose and bit her lips together with a desperate effort at silence. She kissed Gray's ears.

She had never dared to kiss a wolf as proud and royal as Gray.

Every minute fresh sobs racked Feo's throat and chest, but she beat them down so that they could not shake the wolf where she lay.

Black came and sat on the other side of Feo, and breathed wolf breath into her hair. White stood guard.

Feo and Gray lay side by side until sunrise. Feo's body

went from cold to agonizing to numb. Shivers ran through every inch of her skin, but she clenched her fists.

The wolf began to move her shoulders as the dawn came. Her movements were very slow.

Feo whispered, "Please don't go. Wait until we find Mama. She'll know what to do."

Gray gave a little panting, whistling noise. Feo gulped in breath. "You can't die. I love you. I love you too much for you to die."

She focused on breathing onto the wolf's nose, so that the air the wolf inhaled would be soft and warm and familiar. She screwed up her eyes so that they could not leak. Gray had never liked tears, nor rain: only snow.

The sun rose over the forest in splashes of red and purple. When the light hit the wolf's closed eyes, she must have felt it, for her hind legs quaked with the pain as she heaved herself to her feet.

"Gray!" Hot hope surged into Feo's chest, and she sprang forward to help. "Are you feeling better?"

But Gray's footfall was not steady. The wolf paced to the edge of the forest and dropped there. She arranged her great paws to point north. Her muzzle, rough and soldierly, faced the dark and the journey ahead. Her chest rose, and fell.

And did not rise again.

Feo curled up into a ball and stuffed handfuls of hair into her mouth, and roared into the snow.

The pup was nuzzling at her neck, mewing feverishly, trying to get back close to warmth, but when Feo tried to reach out to scoop him nearer, she found she could not move. Misery and guilt had frozen her joints where ice and snow could not.

The pup stumbled away from her toward Gray. When he reached the body, he clambered up onto her side, nuzzling at her jaw. It seemed to take him several moments before he realized something was wrong. He sniffed the blood. He gave a tiny, piccolo growl. And then he set back his head and howled.

Feo's hands shook so hard they lifted her gloves off her fingers. The pup's first real howl was thin and high. It made Feo want to cover her ears or to scream. But she sat on her hands and kept her eyes open.

"I'm so sorry, Gray," she whispered. "I'll kill him."

Slowly, she got to her knees. The trees and wind together sang a nothing song.

Black and White howled too, then. The sound pulled down icicles from the trees. It was rougher and more ragged than any howl Feo had heard. It sounded of things lost and not regained. Feo crawled over to Black and knelt with her head against his chest, and, dizzy and exhausted, she wept as if the world itself had broken.

Marina had always said that the Russians, of all nations, know best how to meet death. You treat your wounded, bury your bodies. You cry, and you sing, and you cook. You do these things not for yourself but for the people left behind.

In this case, for two grown wolves and a wolf pup with a runny nose and a shiver, there was nothing to cook, but Feo shared out some of the dried elk in her pack. She ate some snow. She wiped her face. She retrieved her knife from where it had fallen, tested the edge with her thumb.

Then Feo began to dig using her gloved hands. Digging through the snow was not difficult, but every inch of her body ached, and her arms were slow and unfamiliar. The thought of what her mother would say when she knew was terrible; it sat blackly in her insides.

Soon Feo's gloves met earth, earth frozen solid and harder than rock. She sat back and wiped sweat and snow and dirt across her face. White seemed suddenly to understand what she was doing; the wolf edged Feo aside with her bloody muzzle and set her claws into the earth. Black joined her. At first each went straight down, two separate holes in a row—and Feo couldn't think of a way of showing them what she wanted. Cautiously—she did not know what sort of blood thoughts they might be having—she nudged Black and thumped her glove at the untouched earth between their holes, collapsing it.

Feo paused, and warmed a little snow in her mouth for the pup to eat. She felt very old and tired, more than she had felt in her life before. She had never been more ready to kill.

She scratched Gray's name into a tree and, below it, Rakov's. Below that, just in case he returned—just in case—she scratched: "We are coming."

Gray was far heavier in death than Feo expected, and she staggered sideways, but it would have been wrong to drag her. At the last moment her arms gave out and she half lowered, half dropped her into the grave, then pushed the earth back. The wolves let her. Feo stamped on the earth and kicked snow on top, ignoring the numbness in her feet.

The snow was mixed with mud, and it was obvious someone had been there, but when she felt sure the smell of blood had gone and no stray foxes would come and find Gray, she sat down on top of the grave, stroking the disordered fur of the pup, and rocked backward and forward with her chin on her knees. The pup's tired keening kept time. As she rocked, Feo sang a lullaby mothers sing to newborns.

Black and White lay around her in a ring, tail to nose and

still as stones. Their eyes were open. Surrounded by their warmth, Feo had a last waking thought of small victories: There will always be things that money cannot buy, things that you have to earn. It seemed right that Gray, the bravest creature Feo had known, should have her grave marked with something beyond the reach even of the tsar: a wreath of wolves.

TWELVE

Feo had been riding on Black's back for what felt like several hours when they first spotted the castle. Or rather, not a castle, but the ghost of one.

The gate was black and gold, wrought with angels and eagles, and stretched as tall as two men. Set on top of the only hill for miles, it was devastatingly imposing. "But I am not," said Feo, "going to be intimidated by architecture."

Feo found a stick and poked it through the gates to test the snow's depth: It had gathered waist high on the tree-lined path—"A winter's worth," whispered Feo—and except for the bird marks there were no footprints. The chain on the gate, when Feo scraped the snow off, showed a year's worth of rust.

"What do you think?" she asked Black. "Does it smell safe?"

There was no wind. Feo pushed her hair back and brushed the snow out of her ears, but no sound of any living thing came to her. Around them were snow-thick fields, and the trail the wolves' feet had left.

The wolves slid between the bars of the gate. Feo leaned through and balanced the pup on Black's back. "Don't run anywhere, please," she whispered, and then to the pup, "and don't pee on his head."

With both her hands free, it should have been easy for Feo to climb over the spiked railings, but her whole body ached and she tumbled the last meters. The snow broke her fall, though she ate more of it than she would have liked. Her body was slipping out of her control, she thought: She needed somewhere safe to sleep. She would stay only long enough to recover her breath, to make a plan, and they would be on their way.

The fire, as Alexei had said, had not been recent. The trees looked as if they had once been sculpted into the shapes of animals, but now they were sprawling, monstrous shapes, and thickly frosted. Nobody had cleared the autumn leaves before the snow came. Feo sniffed the wall as she approached: The soot barely smelled at all. The castle was a long, low rectangle, with turrets at each side and two balconies, both crumbling and dripping with icicles. The stones were tawny and gray—wolf colors—streaked with the fire's black, and the pillars on each side of the doors were caked in soot.

Feo lifted the pup off Black's head, where he was squeaking and getting his paws in Black's eyes, and put him on her shoulder. "This," she said, "will do."

She struggled through the snow, looking for broken windows at floor level. She found none, so she smashed the compass bowl against the floor-to-ceiling window at the back, and Black followed her through. She took in a high-ceilinged hall with soot-blackened wallpaper and a blackened chandelier chain with no chandelier, but her eyes were aching. She half crawled up the marble staircase, turned into the first room, which turned out to be a study full of smoked books, and curled up on the floor.

"I won't sleep for long, I promise," she said to the pup. "Please don't chew my shoes. Or—that's difficult, I know— please don't eat the walls. I think the soot would be bad for you." The pup pawed at her chin. As gently as she could, Feo pushed him away. "I need to close my eyes, just for a second, *lapushka*."

Feo woke to find her nose buried in someone's fur. She had woken up like that several hundred times before, and for a moment there was just the peaceful smell of animal skin and firesides—and then, suddenly, the remembrance of the past few days came rushing down over her.

The voice inside that said "Mama!" woke up again.

Feo jumped to her feet, wincing at the recently defrosted feeling in her toes, and shook herself. White shook herself too, and stopped biting at her bandages. Feo laid a hand on her friend's head, and together they began to explore the mansion.

The left side of it was gutted out, exactly as she had imagined fire working: Nothing much remained, except the stone carvings. But the right side, which seemed to be made mostly of a large library and the little study she had slept in, was more or less untouched, though empty of anything useful, like guns or chairs or clothes. The downstairs was similar: a ballroom on the right side, with smoke-smeared green and golden wallpaper that Feo was grudgingly forced to admire, and exquisite but charred velvet curtains. On the left of the staircase there was a burnt-out kitchen—that must have been where the fire started, she thought—and a charred room that might have been anything. A drawing room, perhaps, of the sort Black and White and Gray might have known in their early aristocratic days.

The thought of Gray rose up, and she pushed it down again.

There was a howling from the front hall. Black was trying to summon her.

"What is it?" Feo glanced around for a weapon. Everything movable seemed to have been taken away by the last owners.

"I'm coming!" She picked up one of the half-burnt books from the floor, hefted it in her hand, and stepped into the great marble hall. Black was standing at the smashed window. On the other side was a blond boy wrapped in a green cloak.

"Ilya!" She ran to him, her boots crunching in the glass, and threw her arms around him. He waited a moment, then gave a little shake, like a dog, and she released him.

"You hug hard!" he said, but he was grinning.

"Yes," she said. "I know. I forgot. Sorry. I'm used to wolves. They hug with their teeth."

"Well, don't do that, either!"

"No, I won't. Sorry."

"Don't be sorry. Feo, we found you!"

"Here, come in. Not that bit, though—here, where there's no glass. Who's we?"

For one giddy moment she thought he meant Gray, but that was impossible.

He was pirouetting around the hall. "Alexei said you'd be here! And I knew you'd be all right. People should listen to me more!"

"Ilya, I have to tell you something—"

But he shook his head. "I can't stop! I've got to make sure the others don't miss the castle!" He turned a somersault on the spot. He was obviously in a holiday, leapfrogging mood. "I said you'd be here!"

"What others?"

"Them!" He pushed her to the broken window and pointed.

Feo looked. There were only the fields, a few empty summer dachas, and the white humps of trees. But a noise came to her on the air—not wolves, she thought. Not wind. Not snow. Something else: Something she had never heard before.

Over the horizon came a snaking line of children—the children from the village—skiing, running on snowshoes, waving sticks and bats and hands, waving at her. Behind them she saw Alexei's dark head, with Clara on his shoulders and an ax in his hand.

The children's cloaks and coats—blue and green and red—cast colored light on the snow, bright as her paint box at home. The little ones were singing a marching song. Alexei conducted with his ax. Sergei whooped war cries and waved at the castle with both hands as he came.

"The adults didn't want them to come, so I made a

diversion—I danced, actually. I think they thought it was a bit odd, because they were eating, but they watched—and we got away! We've come to get your mother back! I told them the whole—" Ilya broke off. He stared.

Feo—the wolf witch the other soldiers had talked about in awe, who had not cried when her mother was snatched away and who had only scowled at snowstorms and guns and ice-cold nights—was shaking.

"Feo?"

Feo shook her head; she couldn't speak. The moments in which the world turns suddenly kind can feel like a punctured lung. She stood in the marble hall and cried until tears flooded down her nose and chin and dropped onto the heads of the two bloodstained wolves at her feet.

It took hours to get everyone inside and to let them explore, and to dust the soot off the little ones—hours, too, for Ilya to stop shaking and repeating, "He shot her? He shot Gray?"

The two of them walked through the house, avoiding the others, swapping ideas for what they would do to Rakov when they saw him.

At last they marshaled the little ones and herded them into the ballroom. There was a small gang of little ones, made of two well-wrapped-up seven-year-old boys, Gregor and Yaniv, and two sisters, Vasilisa and Zoya, huge-eyed and dressed like snow elves in white coats. Sergei shepherded them into place, supremely superior at eight years old—together with Bogdan, still sniffing, Clara and Yana, and Irena, a girl of about fourteen with wary eyes. Ilya produced black bread from his sack, and some piroshki, buns stuffed with roast pork. There was quite a lot of grabbing and stamping, and then suddenly everyone was sitting on the floor of the ballroom, staring up at Ilya and Feo and Alexei, chewing and listening.

"I vote we storm the city," said Alexei. "The adults are still debating about what to do: They might be weeks. We're going to do it *now*—or, at least, soon."

"But what about Feo's mama?" said Yana. "It's her we've come to rescue!"

Alexei looked as though he'd forgotten about that for a moment. Then he recovered his poise. "Exactly! We're doing both at once: We're going to make enough noise and mess and chaos to give Feo time to break into Kresty Prison."

"We're going to bite the guards!" said Sergei, baring his gums. "Like the wolves, only harder."

"I was thinking of something a bit more sophisticated than that," said Alexei. "Not that biting isn't very much the right kind of thinking."

He had been leaning against the doorway, and now he pulled himself up on the door frame and swung his legs, as if kicking an invisible soldier. "It's not just us out in the country who hate Rakov and his men. He's sent his requisitioners into the city. There are people waiting for a reason to fight. We could give them one."

"What, though?" Feo sat on one of the windowsills of the ballroom, the pup in her lap, the wolves at her feet. White was chewing on a half-burnt curtain. "Is Mama the reason to fight?"

"Sort of. But I meant you and the wolves. Picture it, Feo! You, standing on a pillar—there's bound to be a pillar somewhere—telling what you did to him! A ski straight in the face! And then you lead the little ones in, like an army, march through the streets, with the wolves running ahead. Other kids will join us!"

"Do they know how to march?" said Ilya. He was sitting with his chin on his knees, still giving the occasional post-crying hiccup, but his voice came out firm. "It takes time. I should know."

"We'll train them!" said Alexei. He punched the air as he spoke, and his enthusiasm swept over them. "Wait until I've taught Vasilisa and Zoya to bite! We can be fierce! You'll see—and we'll start first thing tomorrow."

"I need to go soon, though," said Feo. "It's Monday."

"The little ones are too tired," said Yana. "Tomorrow."

Feo thought about saying, "I'll go alone," but the remembrance of the woods last night was still too bitter. "All right," she said. "Tomorrow. We'll take the wolves. They might help in the jail."

"They won't let a pack of wild wolves into the center of the city."

"Half wild," said Feo.

"They might not let *any* of us into the city," said Yana. "They're stopping people at the gates. Rakov's nervous. They're stopping anyone who looks like they might be an agitator: which means anyone who isn't a duke or a soldier."

"We could climb the walls!" said Sergei, kicking the wall for good measure.

"You can't even climb the old oak, Sergei," said Yana. "Anyway, they'd shoot anyone climbing in, wouldn't they, Alexei?"

Feo had ducked behind her hair to think better. Now she emerged. "I think I've got an idea." The idea fizzed in her stomach and ran, tingling, down to her fingertips. "Can anybody sew?"

There was a flurry of "Whats" and "Whys."

"You're going to *sew* at Rakov?" said Alexei. "That's not really a classic attack strategy, Feo."

"Truly, I promise! This is the best idea I've ever had."

Eyebrows were raised.

"I know how to get into the city! Some of us, at least. You said they don't let in agitators; they don't let in people who look ragged. But we all know only aristocrats can afford wolves. So—what if we pretend to be rich? What if I use the wolves as camouflage?"

Ilya was staring at her, and his stare was not impressed. "Don't panic, all right, at what I'm about to tell you: Feo, you've gone mad."

But Alexei strode forward, slapped Feo on the back, and laughed his whooping laugh. Black and White growled, warningly, but it only made him laugh harder.

"Do you hear that? That," he said, "is what a real idea sounds like. That is the sound of Rakov falling."

THIRTEEN

A lot of people, it turned out, could sew, or at least claimed they could. The next morning Yana, Bogdan, and the two little sisters, Vasilisa and Zoya, pulled down the curtains, borrowed Feo's knife and the pin from the compass—"It works as a needle," said Yana, "if you don't mind big stitches"—and fell to work.

"It doesn't need to be perfect, remember," said Feo. "Most of it will be under my cloak." Then she was pulled away again; that whole day, wherever she went, hands were tugging at her arms, ankles, cloak. It gave her an unexpected flicker of warmth in her chest and hands.

Sergei was asking for permission to lead a party outside,

toward the outhouse, to search for weapons.

"But don't kill each other," said Feo, "all right? Not even as practice."

Irena rapped on the wall for attention. "You know what's more important than a dress? Shoes. You can't wear boots. Not if you're supposed to be a countess."

"Yes, I can! Nobody will see!"

"But if they *did*."

Everyone looked at Feo's boots. They were charred at the toe and they smelled odd, of wolf pee and blood. They were not the shoes of somebody who flicked caviar at wolves in golden drawing rooms.

"If they did see them, you'd be done for."

"Can anyone swap with me, then?" But everyone else had shoes as bad, or worse.

"Could we make her some boots?" said Yana.

"What from? I'll just risk it," said Feo.

"Wait!" said Ilya. He was glittering with sudden excitement. "Now *I've* got an idea! Ballet shoes!"

"Whose, though?" said Feo.

"The Imperial Ballet School!" He began to hop from foot to foot. "Two miles outside the gates!"

"How do you know that?"

He was split-leaping around the room. "I used to watch

through the windows every night! That's how I learned to dance! They throw shoes away sometimes: A real ballerina gets through more than one pair a *week*. I used to find them." He turned a cartwheel. "I'll go now! They know me, sort of—at least, not really, but the servants are used to seeing me outside. It won't take long!"

"How will you get there?"

"I'll borrow Bogdan's snowshoes."

"Oh, will you?" said Bogdan. But one look from Alexei and he nodded. "All right."

"Shall I come too?" said Feo.

"No," said Yana. "We'll need you to try on your dress. But someone else should go to look after him."

"I don't need looking after!" said Ilya.

"Alexei could go," said Feo. "He's the eldest."

Ilya pinkened. His face wrestled with a very badly hidden smile, and he led Alexei down the path, gesturing in the direction of the city. Feo watched them clamber over the gate.

Yana came up behind her. "Who's going with her? Aristocrats your age don't travel alone."

"Ilya, obviously. Alexei."

"But what will they wear?" asked Yana.

"Ilya's uniform will do for him," said Feo. "It's dirty, but you can't tell unless you look hard. Alexei can wear my mother's green cloak—nobody will see if he's not elegant underneath it."

Yana said, "Good. If anyone asks, you can say he's your big brother."

"Second cousin," said Feo. "He looks nothing like me." It was a shame, she thought. It wouldn't be such a bad thing to look like Alexei did: a bit like sun encased in skin. But she had scars on her hands from when Gray was a half-wild pup, and she wouldn't swap them for anything in the world.

A few hours later Sergei and his gang came cascading in from the castle grounds, bubbling and sniffing with excitement.

"Come and see! Come and see."

"What am I seeing?"

"It's a surprise! Where are Alexei and Ilya?"

"Not back yet," said Feo.

But there was a clanging at the gate as two lanky bodies dropped down into the drive and came running. Ilya was waving something in his hands.

"We got some! At least"—he hesitated—"Alexei did."

"Ilya heard music. He got . . . distracted."

Ilya, Feo now saw, was blushing under the snow on his cheeks. "Just a bit. I wanted to watch the dancers."

Feo looked from one to the other. "What happened?

Sergei, you go ahead, we'll be right there." And then, urgently: "Ilya—did something go wrong?"

"He was dancing," said Alexei, "in full view! Outside the ground-floor window! He was *copying* them—those dancers—in plain sight!"

"Did anyone see?" said Feo.

"One person," said Ilya. His cheeks and nose were turning red. "Only one."

"Ilya! You could have been caught!"

"I *wasn't*, though! A man—one of the teachers, I think—he chased us. But it *did* create a diversion." Ilya's voice had a pleading note. "Alexei found these in the rubbish." The shoes were white, a little large for Feo—but that, she thought, would leave room for socks.

"They're a bit worn out, but quite clean. They might have a *tiny* bit of blood inside, but all ballet shoes do."

Sergei came running around the house and sent a snowball at them. "Come on, then! You come too! Everyone has to come!"

"What is it?" said Feo.

Zoya said, "It's a secret. We made a secret for you!"

One of the little boys began, "It's an old—" But Sergei slapped a hand over his mouth. "Shh! That's not how you do secrets!"

Feo was seized by small hands and pulled around the corner of the castle, the little ones wading through the snow, Alexei carrying Clara on one shoulder. Sergei pointed to a space where the snow had been trampled by several small feet.

"There!"

It was a dogsled. Feo had never seen one so lovely: It was made of silvery metal, and the children had polished it with sleeves and rags until it shone. The runners had been oiled and a lantern hung on the handle.

The lantern was painted red.

"Did you do all this?" asked Feo.

"Yes!" said Sergei. "Well, Yana helped a bit."

Yana mouthed over his head, *"A lot."*

"We thought, you can't ride the wolves," said Bogdan. "Tell her, Sergei."

Sergei nodded. "People don't. I've been to the city, and people don't ride wolves."

"Yes," said Feo. She wanted to kiss Sergei; his face was so serious, and so dirty. "I guessed that."

"But you might need to go fast. It's a big city. And the wolves could pull the sled."

"Wonderful!" said Feo. "Thank you."

"Don't hug me!" said Sergei. "Ilya says you hug like a wolf!"

Feo flushed, but forced herself to grin. She made a rush toward him; the little ones squealed, deliriously gleeful, and disappeared round the corner of the castle, followed by Yana.

She stroked the sled. "That's quite something," she said. "Look—look at the handles. They shine. That must have taken them hours—and out here in the snow."

At that moment Yana leaned out the ballroom window.

"Feo," she called. "Come and try the dress on!"

Feo's stomach gave a swoop: If the dress was finished, it was nearly time to go.

Nobody had a hairbrush, but they had made do with their fingers and a toothbrush Sergei had borne triumphantly back from the outhouse. Feo shivered in her underwear in the ballroom while Yana lifted the dress over her head. Zoya pulled a loose thread from the hem.

"She's ready!" called Zoya. "Everybody come see!"

There was a lot of bustling in the hall, and then the ballroom door burst open and the children streamed in, Ilya and Alexei last, whispering together.

Everyone fell silent.

A plait curled around Feo's head and fell, thick as her arm, to the backs of her knees. They had twisted it so the tangles didn't show. She was very pale, but her jaw was set. The dress fell in a simple square from her neck and brushed the ground. It was belted tightly with the silver chain from the chandelier, polished by Clara with snow and her sleeve.

Feo held her shoulders far back and her back straight—"If it feels strange," Yana had said, "you're doing it right"—and her chin high.

"Don't look sideways, either," said Yana. "I went to Saint Petersburg once, and rich people look straight ahead. You have been bred, remember, to know that other people will get out of your way."

The girls had touched her lips with some of the red paint from the outhouse watered with snow, and they were purplish red. The ballet shoes were white and made Feo want to point her toes, and the dress, as she strode across the floor, rustled with the sound of fir trees.

"Oh," said Ilya. "That's quite a lot more impressive than I expected."

Yana gave the dress a final pull and stood back. "We need gold. Countesses wear gold."

"I don't have any gold," said Feo. "I had a gold chain before all this, but not anymore."

"I know!" said Ilya. "There was a stack of Bibles in the library!"

"What?" called Alexei. But Ilya had gone. "We don't really have time for praying!"

Ilya was back minutes later, carrying an armful of half-burnt books that came up to his chin. He was not, as far as Feo could tell, in a praying kind of mood.

"The gold lettering! Look—see—it comes off under your fingernail!"

Everybody fell on the books. The idea seemed to make the little ones giddy.

"*God* could arrest you for this," said Sergei. "This is *better* than murder."

Feo rubbed a little of the gold on her finger and touched it to the outside corners of her eyes, and eyelids, and fingernails.

They had more than enough: Feo put a little on Black's eyebrows and some flakes on White's ears. The wolves, after all, were her disguise, she thought: They deserved some war paint.

At last the children stood back, leaving Feo in the middle of the ballroom, the two wolves at her side.

"That," said Alexei, surveying their handiwork, "is the stuff that fairy tales are made of."

The snow was melting that evening as Feo drove the sled into Peter's Square.

A crowd of children had gathered to beg for coins outside the ballet, and they stood, looking up at the sky and down at the girl. The not-snow was almost as extraordinary as the child.

Almost. The girl would have been extraordinary whatever the weather. A blood-red cloak, freshly washed, flapped behind her. Her forearms, from elbow joint to wrist, were covered in scratches and bruises, but her eyes were gold. The set of her chin suggested she might have slain a dragon before breakfast. The look in her eyes suggested she might, in fact, have eaten it.

The boy sitting on the sled, dressed in a soldier's uniform, had a look of determination you see not in habitual adventurers, but in people who have only recently discovered that they are brave. The young man stumping behind, wrapped in green velvet and fur, had covered most of his face. But the mouth could be seen below the hood, laughing.

But what was really extraordinary—what was making the crowd of children stare and whisper—was the pair of wolves she drove before her. They shone with sweat and ice, their backs were humped with muscle, and they were speckled with gold.

This, then, was a jail. Feo had never seen one before, though she had read descriptions of them. It was surprisingly large and beautiful: four great red-brick wings shaped like a cross around a central lookout post. It was loud too: the shouts of prisoners, occasional laughter, occasional groans. Feo shivered and prayed that the groans did not belong to Mama.

The passage through the city gates had been made easier by the fact there were no adults; only Alexei, and he, lounging against the gate, looked neither adult nor child: the offspring of a war god and a sapling tree. Probably, Feo thought, people just didn't suspect children. It had taken half an hour to find the jail: Ilya's sense of direction, he admitted, was not wolflike. They stopped around the corner of the jail to confer.

"What do you think?" Feo peered at the guards, and at Ilya. "Do I act haughty or sweet?"

"Haughty with the gate guard, I think."

"Yes," said Alexei. "They won't care about adorable: They're sentries. Adorable works best on unobservant people. Look confident."

Feo nodded. Her "confident" face felt a lot like her "scowling" face, but it would have to do for now.

The wolves padded up to the stone arches over the jail. There were men in uniform marching across courtyards.

Feo looked at the guard: She let her eyes travel up from his boots to his beard. She thought about lisping, but discarded the idea.

"Good evening, man," she said.

Behind her, she felt Alexei nod.

"Um, my father said I should wait for him inside," she said.

"Who?"

"My father."

"Yes, but who is your father?"

Feo said the first name that came to mind. "Count Wolfovich. And this is my cousin. And this is his . . . pet soldier."

Ilya glared.

"I don't know the name," said the guard. "I can fetch someone, though—just a second."

"My father is the tsar's second cousin," said Feo quickly. She forced astonishment into her voice. "He would be surprised to hear you don't know of him. And . . . um . . . his surprise is often painful for those who feel it."

"I—" The guard hesitated, glancing over his shoulder.

"I was told the guards were properly educated. But if not, I will simply tell him—"

"No need for that, miss!"

"Let us pass, please."

"Of course. No need to mention this, miss. And what beautiful wolves."

"Thank you," said Feo. "I know."

"They make such good pets," he said, his ingratiating smile lingering on Black's gold-flecked fur.

Feo moistened her lips. The wolves felt her quiver, and Black's hackles rose. "Yes," she said. "Don't they just."

"Well, you probably know the way. You can wait in the warden's library. Fourth floor of the central tower. Stay away from the cells."

Feo was not sure about the fourth floor—wolves do not like stairs, and Ilya was making meaningful faces at her—but there seemed no choice. The stairs were marble with thick brass balustrades, and the wolves' claws made a *tap-tapping* on them as they climbed. It sounded, to Feo, loud enough to summon every soldier and prisoner in the place.

Nobody did appear, though, as they made their way up. On the second floor, just next to the staircase, there was a marble alcove. It had a statue of an austere-looking saint in it, and a small marble bench. Feo ducked into it. The glory of having made it this far rose up in her throat, and she had to force herself not to giggle.

"Ilya!" she said. "Ilya, what were your faces trying to say?"

His face was red, but not with glee. He glared at her. "I was trying to say we should be going to the wings of cells, not up the central tower."

"Well, I didn't get that. Try to make your faces more specific next time."

"Faces aren't specific things! Faces are *general*!"

"My faces are quite specific, actually. And your faces said, specifically, 'Someone is making me kiss my great-aunt.'" She grinned at him.

"Which way now?" Alexei's voice cut across the bickering. "Ilya?"

"I don't know," said Ilya. He avoided looking at the older boy. "I know there are four wings of cells, shaped like a cross."

"Yes, but which one will Mama be in?"

"I don't know. I thought there might be signs to the women's block. But there's not. I'm sorry."

All the laughter and hope dropped out of Feo's chest. "I thought . . . it would be easy once we were in. I thought we'd at least be able to *see* her."

Ilya said, "I think the South Wing might be the one for women. But . . . I'm not sure."

Alexei, though, seemed unperturbed. "We can't just guess: We only get one try. If we guess wrongly, they'll sound the alarm and we'll *all* end up in jail. Which is not in the plan. So"—he turned to Ilya—"where will the servants be?"

"Why?"

"Servants always know more about the details of a place than anyone else."

"But they won't tell *you*!"

"Actually, I've found," said Alexei, "that people will tell you whatever you want, as long as you're nice enough, and as long as there's nobody else around. And you can usually tell from looking at someone if they're going to be a talker."

"How?" This, Feo thought, was useful information.

"It's in the eyes, and the way the mouth falls. Look out for someone who wears his eyebrows a little higher than most people, and whose mouth is like this." Alexei opened his lips two millimeters and pushed his lips slightly forward. "As if they're always about to speak."

"Then let's go!" said Feo.

"And look out for people who talk fast. Fast talkers often let out information without realizing they're doing it. I should know. I am one."

Nobody stopped them. They paraded down the tiled floor, the wolves' claws clacking like high heels, and nobody batted an eye. It was as if the gleaming wolves acted as a kind of camouflage: They melted into their surroundings. Busy men in groups of two and three pushed past, some of them with wolves of their own, a few of them turning to smile in a fatherly way at the top of Feo's retreating head.

The door to the kitchens was painted white. From behind it came the clatter of washing up, and bursts of singing, and hurrying feet. Alexei ushered them in and, grinning, asked for meat for the wolves.

"Count Wolfovich's orders," he said.

There was a girl dressed all in black polishing the silver.

Feo edged closer. "How long does that take you?"

The girl wore her hair piled high on her head. It wobbled precariously as she polished. "A few hours, miss." Feo studied her. Her eyebrows, as she answered, were high. A talker, perhaps.

"How many spoons is that?"

"More than a hundred here—that's for dinner in honor of the army tonight. There'll be thirty of them, but they get four spoons each."

"What!" Feo jibbed, and stopped. She'd been about to ask, "What on earth for?"—but countesses would know. She said, "What—what a task!" and winced at herself. Disguise is not an easy thing. "What are they celebrating?"

"They've arrested a bunch of agitators, miss. Least, that's what they say. Most of them are just homeless folk. But they want them off the streets for General Rakov's visit on Thursday."

"What will they do with them?"

"I don't know. With Rakov, nobody knows. He's got a violent heart, that man." Her eyes widened. "He's . . . not a friend of your parents, I hope, miss?"

"No," said Feo, with complete honesty. "Tell me about him."

"Well, there's some poor woman dragged in from the countryside, too. Rakov's pushing for the death penalty, says it's her fault he's lost an eye." She lowered her voice. "He wants to watch in person."

"But . . . she won't have had her trial!"

"What?"

Feo shook herself. "Um . . . I meant, I hope they're keeping her safe until her trial."

The girl wiped her hair from her eyes in a proud sort of way. "This is the safest prison in Russia, miss."

"And is she . . . is she in the safest wing?"

"Well, there's just the one for women, miss—the North. Barely anyone in it at the moment, but that'll change, the way General Rakov's going."

"Fascinating," said Feo. She nearly said "thank you," but stopped herself just in time. Countesses, she decided, were probably not the "thank you" sort of people.

It took all the self-control Feo had not to sprint straight out of the kitchens and down to the North Wing of the jail. But Alexei kept a strong hand on her arm as they left and pushed her and Ilya into an unused library.

"She's in the North Wing!" cried Feo. "She's just down there!" She shook off Alexei's grip and pirouetted. "Let's go!"

"We can't go now," he said. "I was talking to the cook— he said there's one guard for every two cells. You wouldn't get *close* to her."

"We'll just have to run fast!" she said. "Come on! She's right there, waiting for me! You'll come with me, won't you, Ilya?"

But the younger boy's face was grave. "We wouldn't make it," he said. "There's no way. We need numbers. We need an army."

Feo stared from one to the other. "I *knew* you'd side with Alexei!"

Ilya turned puce. "It's nothing to do with Alexei! It's *fact*."

Feo sagged. She sat down on the floor next to Black and laid her head against his side. "I just want to see her."

"But, Feo—we *have* an army!" said Alexei. "At home! We

just need to get them ready, and then we can storm the jail. We'll make a diversion, and we'll break out your mama."

"When?" Feo brushed some gold out of her eyes and swallowed hard. She bunched her fists. "Tomorrow?"

"Thursday. During Rakov's visit: They'll all be on parade, or polishing their buttons. *That's* the time."

"How?"

"First," he said, "we need to train our mob. Then we start a revolution."

FOURTEEN

In the half-burnt library the children slept soundly, clustered together under blankets pilfered from their homes. The ballroom, with its marble floor, was too icy to sleep in, but the library was well insulated by books, and the sound of the sleeping children was soothing each time Feo woke with a cry in the night.

Training to be a proper mob began the next morning.

Alexei hustled the children from their beds. The warm fuzz of sleep was still on them, and nobody was pleased to be led into the ballroom, which was as cold as the snow outside. But nobody said no to Alexei. It would be like saying no to a whirlwind.

"Right!" Alexei paced in front of them, his sleeves rolled up, his bangs held back by a band of cloth. "We need to get warm before anyone can learn anything. Nobody can learn with a cold brain."

"I'll light a fire," said Feo. "There's matches in Ilya's pack."

"No!" said Alexei. "We're running thirty laps of the ballroom."

There were some groans.

"Anyone groaning," said Alexei, "spends tonight outside with the wolves."

Feo opened her mouth to object—it seemed unfair on the wolves—but Alexei's face was not the kind that left space for disagreement.

"Listen," he said. He spread out two hands. "Children are smaller and weaker than adults. It's just a fact. So we need to be faster, and braver. That's math. You don't have to run, Feo, unless you want to. You won't be in the mob."

Feo ran anyway. At first it was fun to outrun everyone: streaking past the little ones, past Ilya's lolloping stride, which involved a lot of elbow movement—he would be even faster if he moved more with his ankles and less with his knees, she thought, but resolved to tell him when Alexei was not there—and past Alexei himself. Alexei looked a little startled as she overtook him: He sped up, shoulders forward, his shirt coming untucked as he ran. Feo sped up too. He grunted as she passed him again, then turned his attention to Yana and Irena. "You're running," he called, "like someone's grading you on neatness. Run like wolves are after you!"

Feo refrained from pointing out that running if wolves are after you is more optimistic than useful.

"All right!" he called. "That's enough. Everyone sit on the floor. We've got dried apples somewhere—Vasilisa, will you hand them out?" And then, under his breath, to Feo, "Who taught you to run like that?"

"Mama." Feo looked at her hands. "If you grow up running in snow, running on waxed wood or stone is easy. I grew up thinking wolf pace was normal. To them, I'm slow."

Feo excused herself from fighting. She had had enough of blood for the time being. She sat on the windowsill with the pup in her arms, feeding him milk from the tip of her finger.

Alexei paced, lionlike, among the children as they sat looking up at him. "We have one advantage when we reach the jail—the guards can't shoot children in front of other people. At least," he said, "they can, but people seem to like it less." He looked pointedly at Sergei, who was biting his toenails. "I honestly have absolutely no idea why.

"So, we're going to practice attacking. When we're in

Saint Petersburg, you'll be too frightened to think: You'll hesitate. But if your muscles know exactly what they're supposed to be doing, they'll do it even if your brains are scared. We're training to make your bodies braver than your brains, you see? That's what soldiers do."

"But I won't *be* scared!" said Sergei.

"Last year, when lightning hit the oak tree, you wet the bed," said Bogdan.

"I did *not*!" He looked, outraged, around his gang. "The rain came through the ceiling."

"Just onto your mattress and nowhere else?"

"Quiet, all of you!" said Alexei. He rapped on the wall, but it didn't stop the chatter. "Listen—listen to me!" He was obviously struggling. Children were even harder to marshal, Feo thought, than wolves. She grinned and gave a tiny howl. Black picked it up immediately. The windows shook.

Everyone jumped several inches. Quiet dropped on the room.

"*Thank* you. So!" said Alexei. "What was I saying? Oh, yes—there are lots of things the guards have that we don't. They're trained. They have guns. But we're fast, and light. We can climb up drainpipes; they can't follow. Our feet make less noise. They'll have forgotten things they once knew—they'll have forgotten how to bite, and how to spit, and how to use their nails. And we're not going to fight like gentlemen—you understand?"

Feo raised her eyebrows.

"*Or* like ladies," he added. "When we get inside the jail, there are no rules. You can pull hair and kick them in the groin and bite earlobes, all right?"

"Can we tie them up?" said Sergei.

"Yes," said Alexei. "Good. Yes!"

"Can we pull out their beards?"

"Yes. Although, actually, I think beards are quite well anchored. But you can try."

"Can we kick people in the shins? I've always wanted to, but Mama says they break easily."

Feo, from her windowsill, grinned. She knew what Sergei meant: Shins were so tempting.

"Yes!"

"Can we—"

"Yes! Everything, yes. Remember: The most vulnerable places are nose, groin, shins, and eyes."

The children stared up at him. Every single face was blazing with pleasure.

"What weapons will we have?" asked Irena. She looked a lot like Alexei, Feo thought, though less right angled and less disconcertingly beautiful; perhaps she was another cousin.

"I'm not sure yet. We're going to have to see what we can make. But for now," he said, "we're going to practice."

By the time the afternoon sun had made its way into the ballroom and thawed some of the frost that lined the windows, Feo was exhausted. But it had been a shining kind of morning.

First, Alexei cut the sleeves off their shirts—"It frees your arms," he said—and wound them into ropes.

Then he sent out expeditions to cut down branches from the oddly shaped bushes and trees—waiting until snow was falling at its heaviest, to mask their prints.

They sharpened flint from the gravel path into knives, and bound them to the tips of sticks for spears, wrapped securely with scraps from their shirts.

Alexei lined them up—from the smallest five-year-old to Yana, soft skinned and bold and brave, at the far end—and taught them to parry, to stick and twist.

"Jab," he said. "No, grip with your thumb, Sergei. Good, Zoya!"

Feo and Ilya, who Alexei had exempted from training— "Soldier and wilder," he said, "I've seen you with a knife, Feo"—sat by the fireplace and made more weapons.

Feo warmed some yew she found over the fire until it was supple again. "Look!" She tugged some string from the curtains.

"A bow. Do you know how to make arrows?"

"I think they taught us in the camp," said Ilya, "but I wasn't listening. That was the day I worked out how to handspring."

Every twenty minutes or so Alexei used Feo and Ilya as targets for flint-throwing, and they would be forced to duck and jump, or retaliate with whatever they had around them. Trying to ignore him didn't work.

Alexei hustled the children into doing push-ups, helping the littlest ones, nudging the older ones with his toe. He ran up and down the ranks, panting and shouting orders. "Quiet, Sergei! You can talk later. For now you can nod, but only when I say so."

"Being around him is like being around an alarm clock. One that doesn't turn off," said Ilya. There was admiration in his voice. Alexei, Feo thought, went from zero to fiery in thirty seconds. He seemed to have no middle range: only hurry, anger, bossiness, laughter, and sleep.

"It's not that he's not good," Feo said to Black, as dusk fell. "He is good. It's that there's so *much* of him."

Feo, used to days of silence with her wolves, of whispers and fur and snowfall, found the roomful of children took some getting used to. The little ones came clamoring to her after their training sessions, pretending to be wolves and biting her knees, tying and untying her shoelaces, stroking the pup as he lay in her arms, begging to plait her hair. But when Alexei called, they returned without needing a second call.

"It would be easier to dislike him," said Ilya, "if he weren't so beautiful."

"He's like weather," said Feo. "You can't dislike weather."

But it was Feo, not Alexei, who taught Yana and Irena and Ilya to fist fight. Nobody, she explained, can grow up with wolves without learning to understand and measure pain.

"Fighting is as much about knowing when *you're* hurt as knowing *how* to hurt," said Feo. "There are certain kinds of pain you can safely ignore, and some you can't." They wrapped their hands in cloth and learned to punch. "Don't tuck your thumb into your fist or it'll break. Twist your fist as you make contact. Make your knuckles sharp."

That evening, Vasilisa and Zoya came running from their visit to the outhouse, full of news.

"There's a greenhouse! It's only got nettles, but they're alive!"

Feo allowed herself to be led by both hands out to the greenhouse. The glass was smoke stained, but there were indeed whole beds of nettles, nettles sprawling in pots and climbing to the ceiling, growing where flowers once had been. Feo whooped. "Here—don't get stung. Wrap your hands in your cloaks. Can you carry some of these pots inside? Wonderful!"

The girls seemed tiny, but they piled the pots in their arms. Feo grinned down at them. They had the same eyes, she thought, as the pup: young and clever. "Thank you!"

The rest of the plants Feo pulled up by the roots. Keeping her hand safely inside her cloak, she scrunched the leaves into a ball and welded them together with a little snow.

"If you got that in the face," she said, "you wouldn't be able to see for at least a few minutes—maybe a few days."

Vasilisa and Zoya gave thin, piping cheers from behind their pots of nettles.

"You two are far, far tougher than you look," said Feo.

The girls turned pink.

"People usually are, I suppose," she went on. "If you need them to be. Come on. Alexei smuggled some potatoes out from your village, and we're roasting them with bacon."

They were just settling the little ones down for the night when Feo first felt the jolt of something wrong.

"Listen," she said. Ilya, settling a blanket over Clara, stopped midtuck. But there was only the snuffling of the children's breath.

Then she heard it again: the crunching of snow.

Footsteps.

"They've found us," she whispered.

"What is it?" asked Clara, half awake.

Feo held her finger to her lips.

"What's going on?" asked Alexei. He had been standing in the window seat, the better to keep watch. "Are they coming?" He tore a strip off the curtain and wrapped it round his fist.

"Can you hear that?" asked Ilya.

More footsteps, the shaking of the iron gate at the end of the drive. "That's a person," said Feo, looking out the window. "I can't see anything, though. It's too dark."

"Rakov?" said Alexei.

"I don't know."

"You should leave, Feo," said Ilya. "Take the wolves now and go."

"Yes! We can hold them off," said Sergei.

"You've never fought *anyone* before," said Bogdan.

"That's why I should start now, while I'm still young," said Sergei.

It took an immense effort not to hug him.

They took branches from the study fire for light and marched down the marble stairs, Feo first, Yana bringing up the rear with Clara on her hip.

Feo looked at the pile of glass from her break-in. "We can make snowballs with glass in them. Who wants to do that?"

Unsurprisingly, Sergei wanted to.

"And, Bogdan, you've got good aim. Will you?"

Bogdan blushed and sniffed and nodded, all in one fluid motion. "All right."

"And there are nettles in the hall. Put them in the snowballs too. Make a big pile of them, if you can. We'll need lots. Yana, will you stand guard over them? And here— Vasilisa, Zoya—here's my knife. If anyone comes through the window, I'm giving you permission to stab their ankles."

"I'm scared," whispered Vasilisa.

"I know, *lapushka*. Me too." Feo crouched and stared them in the eyes, speaking double speed. "And I don't know where courage comes from. But I do know that if you can scrape together just a bit, more of it comes without your trying. All right? So you don't need a great lump of bravery: only a tiny breath of it. Can you do that?" They nodded, eyes solemn, hand in hand. "Wonderful!

"I'll be right back!" She ran upstairs: Her bow lay by the fireplace. She snatched it up, slid down the banister back to the hall, and skimmed over the marble floor to the kitchen. Ilya followed, rolling up his sleeves. The kitchen felt arctic, and icicles hung from the ceiling.

"Look!" She pulled off one of the icicles, latched it onto the bow like an arrow. "See?" She pulled them down in handfuls: Some were blunt at the end, some as sharp as pins. She handed the bow to Ilya. "You take this."

"What about you?"

"I've got the wolves. Alexei," she called, "I think everyone should be in the hall."

Alexei's voice rang out. "Everyone on the staircase! Bring a torch!"

The children grouped on the staircase, their hands full of snowballs and burning torches. Feo looked up at them—a band of beautiful would-be criminals—and her nose prickled with love.

And somebody knocked on the front door.

Feo swallowed. She hadn't expected knocking. Ilya pulled back his icicle arrow.

The door swung open.

Ilya sent an icicle shattering against the wall. The laughter that came from the man in the doorway did not sound very military. And the body was tall, lean and strong, gray-haired, and dressed in rich blue satin.

The children let out a battle yell.

Ilya gasped. "Don't attack!" he cried. "Cease fire!"

"This," said the stranger, raising two heavily ringed hands

above his head, "was not what I expected. I was looking for a boy. I seem to have found an army."

He stared up at the children on the staircase, cast into flickering bronze by the fire in their hands; at the wolves, still clad in gold. "Is this some kind of theater?"

"No," said Ilya. "It's . . . a mistake, I think."

A change came over the man, the change that you see at sunrise. He laughed at Ilya, still standing with an icicle fitted into his bow. "Not a mistake at all!" he said. "It was you I came to find."

It took a while to persuade Sergei to stop trying to tuck nettles in the man's socks, and to send the others to bed. The night was well advanced by the time they sat down on the floor of the small parlor room, with its charred pink paper and smiling cherubs on the ceiling, and the burnt piano. Feo had boiled water on the fire and made mugs of sweet nettle tea, which the man held at arm's length, as if it might be contagious. Feo and Ilya sat cross-legged and waiting; the man looked awkward, as if he was more used to armchairs. Black sat in the doorway, a just-in-case glare in his eyes.

"As you may know—as you should know—young man, my name is Darikev."

"Darikev?" Ilya looked from Feo to the man and back again. "Igor Darikev?"

"Who's that?" said Feo.

"That's me," said Darikev. "This seems a rather circular conversation. Young man—when we last met I was chasing you."

"Um. Yes. Sorry about that."

"I was not, as you seemed to think, pursuing with intent to eat you, nor to arrest you."

"So why *are* you here?" said Feo.

"I came to offer this young man a place at my ballet school. Presumably you did not think I came for vodka or coffee? Given you seem to be living on snow and plants here."

His voice, and the smartness of his clothes, had made Feo suddenly shy again, but she managed a whisper. "Is Ilya—is he very good?"

"No," said Darikev. "He's not."

Ilya's face went suddenly white, and he stared hard at the floor. "But you said—"

"He's not good *yet*. But his elevation—"

Feo shook her head. "I don't know that word."

Darikev raised his hand above his head. "The boy has height when he jumps, greater than anyone I have in my company. He has a body built for flying!"

Ilya's white cheeks immediately turned purple. Feo nudged him, and resisted the urge to bite his shoulder with the glee of it.

"So, he'll be famous!"

"Perhaps. Perhaps not." Darikev heaved himself to his feet. "It's hard work, young man. I offer you a place only if you understand that. Some grow rich, many do not. Dancers—they are not always respected. They often find it hard to marry."

Ilya fiddled with his lip. "That's not a problem, for me," he said. "I've always known I wouldn't marry."

Darikev nodded. "And your feet will bleed. Your body will ache, every day. And on the few days that your body doesn't ache, your brain will—understand that! Nobody joins without learning our history, the stories behind our dances, reading, recitation." He waved one jeweled hand into the other. "Hard work always hurts somewhere."

Feo grinned. It sounded so familiar: so much like living with wolves. Ilya grinned back at her.

"But," said Darikev, "it's a living. You will dance for millions of people in your lifetime. If you're good enough, they will never forget you. You will become fluent in a new language. Thousands of children will see your feet talking a kind of language they will long to know. You will unearth other people's dreams for them. Do you hear that, boy—and you, girl? People come away from the ballet knowing more than they knew before. You become strong."

"As strong as Feo?" said Ilya.

"I imagine so. Who is Feo?"

"I am," Feo said softly.

"Ah! The young woman with wolves. I've heard rumors about you. Yes, I imagine so. So—what's your answer, boy? Come back with me? There's a horse waiting outside the gates, and a driver."

Ilya's hand reached out and searched for Feo's: Feo grabbed his tight. He said, "I first saw a ballet when I was six—you said that was when you first wilded a wolf. It wasn't very smart—there were gravy stains on some of the tutus. They wore gloves, and some of them were quite slow. But everything there made sense to me. Like with you and the wolves, and the snow."

"Then what are you waiting for?" she said. Her smile was so huge that she felt it might split her lips at the sides.

Ilya turned to Darikev. "No. I can't," he said. "Not now."

"You need to inform your parents? We can do that. There is a secretary who looks after the students' affairs. We are a business, my boy."

"No—not my father. He wouldn't care. But—I've got to do some things here."

Darikev raised the edge of a perfectly pointed eyebrow. "I have no time for those who are not fully committed, boy. Come now or not at all."

"Truly, it's not that I don't want to—I *can't*."

Feo towed him across the room to the window. "Ilya, *what are you doing*? You have to go. There are enough of us without you."

"Don't you want me? To help? I thought we were . . . friends?"

"Of course I want you!" Feo tried to think of words to explain. None of them fit the special circumstances: of a boy who could dance like a war song and who was scared of the cold and who had followed her for miles without once complaining. "You're in the pack. Me, and Black, and White. And the pup. And you. Gray let you ride her. That makes you one of us."

"Yes," said Ilya. "Well, then. I'm staying, aren't I?"

"But that man's offering you so much. He's offering you *years*. He's offering you a whole life."

"No. If it's one or the other, I choose you and the wolves."

"Do you think Darikev would let you stay a bit longer if I bit him?" she asked. "Or if the wolves did? They would,

I think, if we showed them how. Probably. They'd want to help you."

From just behind her came a roar of laughter. Darikev had stepped soundlessly across the room and stood inches away from them. "No need!" he said.

Feo colored. "It was just a suggestion."

"I'm a superstitious old man," he said. "I choose not to interfere in the business of wolves. If those animals have some need of you, young man, it will be best to go. I can give you three days. Ask at the front door for Igor, and they'll organize everything. You will need a haircut. And I would be grateful if you left the wolves behind. I can show myself out, thank you—as long as there are no nettle-wielding children awaiting me."

Feo slept very little that night. It was barely dawn when she woke the children.

"Wasshappening?" said Sergei. "What happened to the man you wouldn't let us kill?"

"Ilya's . . . dealt with him. Come. Let's go," said Feo. "Let's go and find Rakov."

FIFTEEN

The children who came tearing up to the stone gates of Saint Petersburg on Thursday had faces filled with fear. Their panic was impressive, and had been practiced diligently the night before.

"Wolf! Wolf!" they cried.

"What?" The guards looked around. "Where?"

"There! Behind us!" An attractive young woman of about seventeen, with a tiny girl on her hip, gripped his wrist. "In the trees! Look! Let us in, dear God!"

The soldiers pushed open the gates, and the children streamed through, a dozen of them, led by a girl with men's boots and a red-hooded cloak. A boy with a missing front

216 · Katherine Rundell

tooth shouted something—it might have been, "We're in!"—and quickly had a hand clapped over his mouth, but the guards' attention was on their guns, and on firing at the animals who suddenly veered, as if at a signal or a whistle, and disappeared back into the snow.

"Vermin," said one guard. "That's what the general says. Vermin with big teeth."

It was understandable, then, that they did not recognize the two magnificent gold-anointed animals who came processing past them half an hour later, led on a chain by a young soldier. He saluted as he passed, and they returned the gesture. They did not notice how brightly the boy's face shone with suppressed happiness, how he shivered with restrained joy.

Feo and the others were waiting for Ilya in Peter's Square. The sun struck against the golden domes around them, filling the square with sharp winter light. The crowd of staring children from a few days before was still there, still staring: It was as if they had not moved. Alexei slipped among them, whispering, handing out sticks, telling jokes, slapping shoulders. His grin was larger than ever: He stood sleeveless, bruised, and bare headed in the melting snow.

Feo had unplaited her hair and wrapped herself in her old wolf-smelling clothes, and felt more like herself. Her heart and stomach were surprisingly calm. Black shook free of the chain—which, after all, was only painted string—and ran to her, licking her fists and gnawing on the tops of her boots. Feo had streaked his fur with gold, and White's bandage was gold too.

There was a sudden commotion among the children in the square, some pushing and some shouting.

"Hey!" An adult's hand parted the crowd of children, and Grigory, his beard vibrating with rage, pushed to the front.

"Have you any idea," he roared, lifting Sergei clean into the air, "how much trouble you're in?" He crushed Sergei against his chest. "We've been searching the woods for the past three days. It was Sasha who thought you'd be here. Where have you *been*?"

More adults from the village were pushing through the crowd, snatching up Vasilisa and Zoya, hugging them so tightly that the girls let out cries of pain.

"Uh-oh," said Alexei. "We might have a problem."

But Sasha was pushing her way forward, climbing on a bench and shouting for silence. "Grigory! Be quiet, for once in your life. Listen: We've been insane with worry—but we didn't come to shout at you. We came," said Sasha, "to help. To help Feo. And my maddening little brother. We've come for Rakov. It's about time. We're here to fight."

The cheer that went up from Feo's army was so loud that it shook the clouds.

"Say something," said Alexei. "Feo. They're watching you. We need them. Say something."

"But I'm *embarrassed*."

"You have no right to be," he said. "Being embarrassed is a luxury. Hey!" he roared. "Everyone! Listen to her!"

They pushed her to the top of the steps of the cathedral and stood waiting.

"I don't know what to say," began Feo. "Um . . . thank you all for being here. But—"The weight of everyone's gaze on her was too much. Hot, shameful tears began to fill her eyes. She turned to Alexei, fighting the wobble in her chin. "I don't know *how*."

But the crowd was parting on the steps, hissing and yelping, and up the stone stairs, beautiful and bold, stalked Black, followed by White. They crossed to her and sat, one on each side, their faces turned to her. Feo laid a hand on their heads. She breathed in their wild courage. She brushed away the water from her eyes.

"Alexei wanted me to start a revolution. And I'll try: I'll try until I'm dead. But it won't be me starting anything: Mikail Rakov started all this. Rakov came in the night and burned down our home. He took my mama away, because he was afraid of her. He was afraid that she *wasn't* afraid.

"And then—three nights ago—he shot dead one of my best friends."

There was a hiss from the crowd. A group of men came out of a bar and stood, staring, in the middle of the road.

"She was a wolf." Someone laughed, but Feo kept on. "She was the bravest and the cleverest wolf in the world. And so now I need to be braver, so that the total sum of bravery isn't less. Rakov likes to burn things—we all know that—but she had fire *inside* her, and Rakov's afraid of fire when it's inside living things."

A group of nuns filed past and stopped, wrapping their habits around them in the wind.

"And he's taking our food and homes. And he's taking the people we love. How many people here will have to live every single day a little bit lonelier because of him and his gun?"

One of the nuns cheered.

"And he's taking our future. And the future needs our protection: It's a fragile thing. The future needs all the help it can get."

Sasha shouted something high and indecipherable, and swung Varvara into the air, and the baby squealed.

"Rakov wants to kill my mama. He wants to use today to

take her away from me forever. But I"—she pushed the hair out of her eyes and tried to look tall—"I am the wolf girl, and I am not afraid of him!"

That last part was a lie, but a roar went up around the square.

"He's blind now in one eye because of me. But he's *always* been blind: He doesn't see the facts. The fact that there are more of us than there are of him. The fact that fire in your soul beats fire on the ground. The fact that love always beats fear. And the fact that it helps to have wolves on your side."

A nun punched the air and knocked off the hat of a watching chef.

"I didn't want a revolution. I just wanted Mama. I just wanted things to be like they were. And . . . Alexei"—she grinned at him—"sometimes when you talk about revolution, it's actually quite annoying. That's something I found out—revolutionaries are annoying. But . . . Rakov didn't just come for us, for me and Mama. He took Yana's Paul, and that meant he took part of Yana, too. He took part of Sergei, and Sergei's only *eight*."

"Nine!" called Sergei. "Practically nine! Nine in a week!" Grigory laughed and cuffed his son around the head.

Feo barely heard. "Rakov, he saw no reason not to take the things he wanted. He thought fear was the most powerful thing in the world. He thought fear had the most kick—he thought we'd care more about being safe than being bold. But then … he took my Gray." Feo looked around the great square, at the golden domes around her, at the upturned faces. "And now I'd rather be bold. We've got to say, *You do not get to take anything more*. One person can't do it—not alone—but all of us, us kids, we can take ourselves back. We can take our fear back. And I don't know if we'll win, but we have a right to *try*. The adults, they want us to be quiet and careful, but we have a right to fight for the world we want to live in, and nobody has the right to tell us to be safe and sensible. I say, today, we fight!"

Ilya let out a whoop so loud he went purple and had to be hit on the back by Alexei, which only turned him a deeper indigo. Alexei laughed, and hit him again.

"Rakov doesn't believe in us," Feo went on. "He thinks we'll sit, each of us alone with our hands in our laps, hoping we won't be next. He doesn't believe in our bravery. Let's show him that we are brave as … as wolves!"

The wolves recognized the word and stood, and howled, and over their voices Feo shouted, "Tell Rakov to start saying prayers for the souls he took! Tell him we're coming to end it. We have the land in our blood and fire in our feet, and we're coming to change our stories forever!"

There was a roar: a roar that sounded around the square and down the side alleys and caused the children of the city to prick up their ears and turn their heads, like wolves do when they hear a call in the wind.

Ilya let out a choked war cry. He ran ahead of the crowd, down the streets, and spun to face the jail. "Run and hide, Rakov!" he yelled. "I'm coming to show you that you can't despise me! It's a mistake to call people feeble! It's a mistake that's coming for you, with fists!" He spun on the spot, pirouetting so fast Feo expected to see flames leap from his shoes. Without turning to see if they were following, he began to run.

The crowd set off at a wolf's gallop down the pavement, Feo scrabbling onto Black's back at a sprint, her hair whipping at the open mouths of passersby. Sergei gave a roar, as deep as his eight-year-old lungs would manage, and bounded after her.

Feo sped up, urging Black with her knees. The children charged out onto the main road, streaking down alongside the Fontanka Canal. Feo looked back at the gang on her heels, singing, shrieking, running hand in hand with snow in their eyes: very thoroughly wilded. There was something in their whoops—something louder and more guttural than most—that made other children come running out of side streets to watch as they rushed past. They saw golden wolves, the girl with her flying hair, and the singing, gleeful army of children and adults and dogs, hundreds of people swarming down the streets. Ilya sang Tchaikovsky to Zoya and Vasilisa as they ran.

In one side street a gang of children were hanging out laundry. They dropped it and sprinted after the crowd, waving red underpants in their hands for flags. By the time Feo was rounding the corner to the jail, three hundred people were on her tail.

In front of the jail was the same guardsman as before, and his mouth opened to form the word "Countess?"— but Black barreled straight past him, and the sea of three hundred pairs of elbows and knees knocked him against the wall. Faces were appearing at the windows.

Alexei jumped on a post and shouted at the crowd. "Spread out! Break down the doors! Smash all the windows! Split up! Keep them busy!" It was mayhem. The world went from calm to chaos in sixty seconds. Bogdan dancing on marble staircases, Sergei scrambling up a drainpipe to escape pursuit, a horde of nuns swinging right hooks at the guards. All of them, even the smallest, kept up a roar of noise as loud as a hundred-piece orchestra of fury. Feo slipped past them all, taking the route Ilya had drawn for her in the charred wallpaper the night before. Dozens of guards shoved past her, running in the direction of the riot: Some were still chewing their lunches. One struggled to button his suspenders as he sprinted down the corridor. They ignored her: one lone girl with a pair of wolves, walking as fast as she dared, her head down. As she neared the North Wing, the paint became shabbier and the corridor narrower. Ahead of her she could see iron doors set along the wall. She sped up. Black and White ran at her heels, their noses touching the floor.

Feo rounded the corner and froze. She grabbed the wolves' necks to hold them back. A guard stood alone in the middle of the passage, his pistol pointing at her chest.

"Halt!"

"I'm halted. Look." She held both hands above her head.

"Don't move!"

She swallowed. "You have one gun," she said, "but I have two wolves. Wolves are more painful than guns. Mathematically, I think you should give me the keys and run."

The soldier just stared. She realized suddenly that she recognized him: It was the same young soldier who had brought the elk, all those weeks ago. The underbite was unforgettable. He was staring at her with his mouth sagging loose.

"You're that wolf girl," he said.

"Exactly," she said. She pointed behind her. "They need you more out there"—there was a sound of smashing windows—"than in here. And in here the wolves will eat you. Probably. In fact"—she glanced down at them, at the glint of their teeth—"not probably. Definitely."

The soldier was still hesitating when Ilya came charging down the corridor. Sliding on the marble floor, he flashed straight past Feo and the wolves, and at the last moment he leaped, higher than any dancer in Russia, and smacked both shins into the guard's shoulders. They fell with a shout. Feo darted forward and snatched up the keys and the fallen pistol, fumbling with its weight.

"Now one gun, two wolves," she said. She was shivering with nerves and excitement, but she leveled the pistol at the guard's head. "And one ballet dancer, and one wolf wilder. Go."

The guard scrambled to his feet, cast a look of horror at the wolves, and disappeared.

Feo began to unlock the heavy iron cell doors, throwing them open. The first was empty; the next opened on an elderly woman muttering in French—Feo left the door open but ran on. The next was empty again, just brick walls, a plank bench, and a tin bucket.

"Ilya!" She fumbled with the loop the keys were on. "Take this key, try the next corridor. Do you want to take the gun? I don't trust it."

"Right." Ilya turned the corner and disappeared.

"And be careful!" she called. "He might be anywhere."

Feo threw open another cell door, a fourth, a fifth. And stopped, feeling her stomach peel away and plummet to the floor.

Rakov sat on the plank bench. He was dressed in full military regalia, but his face was swollen and puffy, and his leg was bandaged to his thigh. His skin was the gray of dying things. As he saw her, his one eye widened, and his mouth curved upward in a single line.

Feo's heart stopped working. Her knees melted, and she only just held herself from collapsing on the floor.

"You," he said. "Again."

"You're *hiding*," breathed Feo.

"I had no wish to be dragged before a mob."

"They're not a mob. They're people you hurt."

"They do not understand the great things I have done for this nation." His face, as he got to his feet, was full of disgust. "They do not understand how I have purified it with fire."

Feo heard Ilya crash another door. She thought about

shouting for help, but the noise over their heads was deafening. Nobody would hear.

"You exhaust me." He stepped nearer, looking down at her. Feo had never seen such pitiless eyes. "This seems a sad and tawdry end for a child so young," he said. He cocked his pistol. "But life *is* sad."

"I won't—" began Feo, but Black gave a growl that shook the air. White stalked up behind him and growled too: a duet of pure animal menace. "The wolves. They've recognized you," breathed Feo.

"Wolves do not under—" said Rakov, but as he spoke Black streaked past Feo and leaped at him, champed his teeth deep into Rakov's hand as the pistol fired, and twisted with his jaws. Everything went murky for a moment as Feo was pushed against the wall by White's charging body.

When the world cleared, Rakov was backed into a corner, several yards from his pistol. His lip rolled up in so high a sneer that his mustache and eyebrows seemed ready to meet in the middle.

"You don't know what you're doing. Call those wolves off." His voice was full of confidence. "Idiot child! You don't know what will happen if you lay a hand on me. You will be killed!"

"But you *just* tried to kill me. So that's not a very useful threat."

"You do not understand power, or the way the world works." He looked down at the wolves, clustering nearer. "You wouldn't *dare*."

"I think I do dare," Feo said. Her head was swimming, but she forced herself to edge forward in a half crouch and pick up the pistol, then darted backward. "I think I do understand. I understand a lot more these days. The important parts, anyway."

"Child, if you do not call off those wolves, you will spend your life in prison!"

"I don't think I will," said Feo. "No. Thank you anyway."

"Now!"

"They're half wild, in any case." Far away down another corridor, she thought she heard something. A cry. "I can't always control them."

She heard Ilya give a great joyous roar: a weekend, daybreak, sunlit sound. She swallowed. Her fingers were slippery with sweat now.

"You will be punished!" Rakov backed against the wall. "You cannot kill without punishment."

"*You* killed. You killed Yana's Paul. And the hundreds of people that you burned to death. And the people you left to die in the cold. You killed your own soldiers—the old ones—for a *joke*." And then she spat, hard, on his feet, and he recoiled from her in disgust, pressing against the wall.

"You killed Gray." She pointed the gun at his chest.

"I am a general! I am the tsar's favored officer! The rules are different for me! Think of what it says in your Bible—*Thou shall not kill.*"

She looked at him. A vein was jumping on his forehead. His eyes were hard and staring. There was no doubt in them, and no regret.

Feo looked at the wolves, the sharpness of their hackles and the anger in their spines and shoulders.

"Wolves don't read the Bible," she said. "It's up to them." She held her breath as she walked out of the room and down the passage—then she dropped the gun and broke into a run and tore up the stairs, slipping on the marble floor, down the next corridor, following the sounds of laughter. She rounded the corner. At the end of it, hand in hand with Ilya, stood a tall woman with a four-clawed scar circling one eye. Her face was built on the blueprint used for snow leopards and saints.

Marina let out a cry as she bent and opened her arms, and as Feo cannoned into them, the ache in her heart that had said "Mama!" said "Home."

It was several hours before Feo and her mother were able to talk, just the two of them and the wolves. The news of Rakov's fate spread quickly to the men and women of the city. When it reached Peter's Square, the roar that went up was not just from Feo's army: Imperial soldiers joined in, tearing off their gold buttons and tossing them into the air like confetti.

Feo and her mother walked slowly, hand in hand, past marching masses, past a wildly beaming Alexei, making a speech from the top of a handy pillar, and past Ilya, dancing a wild Cossack dance with a crowd of boys in the street; past Clara, sitting on Yana's lap with the wolf pup lying in her arms like a doll—Feo scooped him up, promising to bring him back to visit—and past children's hands that reached out to touch Feo's red cloak for luck. They walked through the unguarded gates of the city, and the noise of singing and fighting faded.

Feo showed her mother the sled and the gold still adhering to Black's eyebrows. "It's book gold," she said. "It lasts a long time."

They stood in the snow, their backs to the churning city. Behind them, a revolution was beginning.

"Where to, my darling?" said Marina. "We can go anywhere now. Back to the woods? South to Moscow?"

"I think," said Feo, "I'd like to sleep. There's a place I know. And I'd like to eat." She realized suddenly that she was starving. "And then tomorrow, I think we should let the wolves decide."

Once upon a time, many years ago, there was a dark and stormy girl.

She lived with her mother in a ruined castle, burnt black outside but shining clean inside. It smelled always of spices, of hot stews, and of the reassuring smell of drying animal.

The girl's bedroom was in the west tower. She had painted the windows with all the colors in her box of paints, so in the evenings light shone out gold and red onto the castle grounds.

In the room next to hers was a bed that was slept in only during holiday months. Ballet shoes hung above the mirror.

And in the ballroom of the castle there lived three wolves. One was white, one was black, and the third, much smaller than the other two, had patches of both colors; his chest, where his heart lay, was gray.

ACKNOWLEDGMENTS

I'm deeply grateful to the following people:

To David Gale and everyone at Simon & Schuster, for such endless kindness. To Ellen Holgate, my UK editor, whose wit and patience I had until now believed existed only in fairy tales. To my wonderful agent, Claire Wilson. To Philip Pullman and Jacqueline Wilson, whose books lit my childhood and whose encouragement has been a gift. To my brother, who has been the first reader of every book I've written. To my mother and father, as ever and for everything. To my friends, especially Mike Amherst, Johnny Howard, Katie Jackson, Daisy Johnson, Jessica Lazar, Daniels Morgan and Rothschild, and Julie Scrase. Lavinia Harrington and Sammy Jay, for our trip to the Arctic circle. Liz Chatterjee, for whisky, and Amia Srinivasan, for wine. Mary Wellesley, whose jokes I have stolen. Miriam Hamblin, who since we met at age ten has been my ideal of generosity. And, most of all, to Simon Murphy, who, among a thousand other wonders, took me to meet my first wolf.